yr. 6-10

And One Was A Wooden Indian

And One Was A Wooden Indian

by Betty Baker

J
Bak

MACMILLAN PUBLISHING CO., INC.
NEW YORK

COLLIER-MACMILLAN PUBLISHERS
LONDON

For my son Christopher.
Because he is.

Contents

1

White-Eye Sign

Hatilshay's eyes did not always see true. Many times a friend, when he drew near, was someone else. Distant wickiups turned into mesquite trees or a kneeling woman became a shadowed boulder. When Hatilshay could not hide his mistakes, he became the target of laughter and jokes. Today, though, Turtlehead would not laugh. Not with his body bruised and cut from their tumble down the rocky slope.

"Your eyes saw false," said Turtlehead. "There was no white-eye soldier."

Hatilshay would not admit it. Not after Turtlehead had asked him to help raid a lonely Mexican ranch and then, three days from winter camp, changed his mind. If one saw or heard bad omens, he was right to turn back. But why hadn't Turtlehead thought to look for signs before leaving? Or consulted his uncle, the shaman of whose powers Turtlehead was ever boasting? The old man would not have approved of two young boys testing their skill alone but he would not have stopped them. That was the way of The People.

Hatilshay never saw omens, good or bad. Or if he did, his eyes tricked him so that he never knew he'd been warned. But this he kept to himself, just as he hid the weakness of his eyes for fear he would never take his place as a warrior of The People.

"I saw a white-eye soldier," he insisted. When he'd awakened Turtlehead just before dawn, he would have wagered every arrow in his quiver that it was true. Now, crouched on the desert and studying the small lonely peak where they'd slept, he was equally certain that he'd seen a yucca plant against the pale sky. As he'd risen slowly to his feet, the yucca had appeared to rise too, like a man's head and hat, behind a rock.

Turtlehead looked up from binding his gashed knee with a strip cut from his loincloth. He pointed his chin at the steep slope. "No white-eye could have climbed up there in the dark and left no sign. We have wasted half the morning searching when there was nothing to be found."

"We have wasted three days traveling when there was no raid," Hatilshay reminded him.

"Would you have gone against the omens?"

"They were your omens, not mine." Before the last word passed his lips, Hatilshay knew what Turtlehead would say. He thought quickly to find an answer.

"Was the white-eye soldier one of your omens?"

"One's medicine is his own." It was the best Hatilshay could do without turning his tongue as false as his eyes.

"If you truly saw him, he was another warning to turn back."

"Who can say about white-eyes?" It was an answer they'd heard often from the shaman.

With great care, Turtlehead stood on his bandaged leg. Then he hung his folded blanket over his shoulder, the way Mexicans carried theirs. Of all The People, only Turtlehead carried a blanket. But then no one else had such a blanket. A large yellow sun was woven into the center of the faded red background. Around it, also in yellow, were strange signs and symbols of lightning. Turtlehead's uncle had given it to him, saying it came from land's end where the sun rose. Turtlehead claimed it had great powers, powers great enough to risk carrying its bulk even when raiding.

The blanket ends were held to his body by a thong tied around his waist. Turtlehead fumbled with the knot, then grunted and inspected his right hand.

"Is it cut?" asked Hatilshay.

"No. I fell on the rocks like this." Turtlehead held his right arm straight out, palm forward. "It is nothing."

Hatilshay waited until ground, sky and air were tested for omens. At last Turtlehead led the way, limping slightly.

Keeping to the cover of low ground and the shadows

of plants, they headed northeast. Across their path rose one of the many small mountain ridges that broke the desert, running from northwest to southeast. Beyond it they must cross more desert, cut by a river that would have little water until the winter rains began. Then they would reach true mountains, rising to meet low clouds and thick with aspen and pine. Now, when snow covered the peaks, The People camped in the low canyons and warmer valleys.

"We can hunt as we cross the ridge," suggested Hatilshay.

Turtlehead nodded. They separated, taking opposite sides of narrow rocky canyons and passes. The sun had begun its downward journey before they crossed the back of the ridge. The far side was deeply shadowed and as empty of life as the other side had been. If they did not eat tonight, Hatilshay would tie a thong around his waist to cut the hunger pains.

As they passed the last boulders and started down the cactus-covered slope, Turtlehead signaled a halt and raised his bow.

The rabbit sat upright, long ears turned to catch sound of them. Hatilshay held his breath until the arrow struck. He watched in amazement as the rabbit bounded off, the arrow shaft thumping its side. Even he could have killed at that distance.

"Turn it from the rocks." Turtlehead ran down the slope, below the rabbit's course. Hatilshay scrambled up, at an angle flanking the lightly wounded animal, to turn it toward the desert and Turtlehead.

The broken ground was not made for a chase. Hatilshay stumbled along the edge of the boulders, uncertain of his next step. For one fearful space he lost the rabbit, then saw it struggling under the broad leaves of a mescal. When Hatilshay reached the plant, only the arrow hung between the thorned leaves.

He freed the shaft and turned to look for Turtlehead, surprised to see him far out on the desert. He did not answer Hatilshay's signal but darted back and forth, pausing now and again to inspect something on the ground. Perhaps he'd discovered the trail of enemies. Mexicans seldom traveled the valley but Bean People often followed the river.

Hatilshay trotted down the slope, moving easily between the widely spaced cacti and bushes. He waved the arrow. Instead of an answering sign, Turtlehead made a throwing motion and sprawled on the ground. Assured by the hump of the medicine blanket, Hatilshay hurried forward. The figure lengthened and thinned. The blanket became cloth packs and beneath them Hatilshay clearly saw a blue uniform. Still he did not stop.

Only a fool walked openly to a stranger but somewhere Turtlehead watched. If Hatilshay turned and ran, what reason could he give for having come so near? Only the truth, that he could not see as well as the oldest man in the village. And like the old men, he would be left with the women when warriors went hunting or on a raid. He would rather die. And he might, for white-eyes were said to kill as often as they gave presents and for as little reason.

Hatilshay's legs trembled and his pace slowed. The People to the west, now led by Mangas Colorado, had been slaughtered by treacherous white-eyes. Yet The People living south in the Chiricahua Mountains traded with white-eye soldiers and had nothing bad to say of them. How could one know about white-eyes? Few in Hatilshay's village had been close to one. Even Turtlehead's uncle, who had traveled west to the salt water and east to a monstrous river, knew white-eyes only through the words of others.

This white-eye, stretched on the ground, made no hostile sign. He did not even move. Was he dead or was this a trap?

Fear dragged Hatilshay's feet while pride and thought of Turtlehead's watching eyes pushed him forward. Like a stone rolled downhill, he walked more and more slowly until at last he stopped. His fear weakened but not enough for him to laugh at the white-eye's position.

The soldier lay holding one end of a stick. On the other end was a cloth spread by a metal hoop. It was surely a hunting weapon, for the white-eye had caught a ground squirrel. Almost caught, for the small animal was held only by the metal hoop pressing down on its striped tail. But the white-eye was also trapped.

He clutched an empty cloth bag in one hand. With the other, he held the stick firmly to the ground. The least movement set the animal squirming and the soldier dared not take his eyes from it. Carefully he placed one knee on the stick and slid his hand forward, pausing each time the ground squirrel wriggled. He would be a long time reaching the animal and Hatilshay wagered he would not get it into the bag.

For Turtlehead's amazement, Hatilshay made sweeping gestures as if speaking to the soldier. He was no closer to the white-eye than Turtlehead had been to the rabbit but his shadow lay before him, three times his height. It betrayed him.

The white-eye spoke softly without turning. "Chulito."

The word was Mexican but it was said that white-eyes and Mexicans had fought a war. More words followed, not Mexican or any other tongue Hatilshay understood. Chulito must be a name, which meant there were others about. The white-eye soldier thought Hatilshay was one of them.

"Chulito!" The soldier motioned backward with the cloth bag. There was no mistaking the command. Hatilshay backed three paces, turned and ran.

Behind the first bush large enough to shield him, he paused to glance back, then ran again. His fourth stop was far up the hillside. He could no longer see if the white-eye had turned to watch him or still crept along the stick to his ground squirrel. Hatilshay chose a path to the nearest boulder and ran for it. He sprawled full length behind it, surprised to discover the shadows had scarcely moved since he'd lost Turtlehead's rabbit. He'd also lost the arrow, though he'd no memory of dropping it. Turtlehead would take it as an omen against hunting.

With a sigh, Hatilshay rose and peered from his hiding place. Though he shielded his eyes and squinted painfully, he saw no trace of the soldier. Had the white-eye moved or had Hatilshay's eyes tricked him again? If they had, then his ears had turned false too, for he'd heard the white-eye speak.

A stone hit the ground beside him. Someone waved from the shadows of a creosote bush back along the ridge. Hatilshay ignored the summons. How could he be certain it was Turtlehead? It might be that Chulito person, a white-eye soldier or just a trick of eyes and ears.

Another stone followed, more badly aimed than the first. Then the figure hobbled from the shadows, dragging his left leg. The hump over the shoulder was familiar. Hatilshay prepared to run if it became something strange, but this time it was truly the medicine blanket. Hatilshay grinned in welcome.

Turtlehead scowled. "Why did you not come to me?"

Hatilshay looked pointedly from Turtlehead's hiding place to the way they planned to travel. "I am farther along the trail."

"But I am wounded."

"You scarcely limped when we crossed the ridge and you ran to help catch the rabbit." Hatilshay immediately regretted mentioning the lost game but Turtlehead was concerned only with his knee. Blood streaked his leg from the bandage to the top of his high moccasin.

"I fell again," he said. "And again it was because of your white-eye friend."

"He is no friend of mine."

"You walk openly to him, as if he was your mother's brother."

While Hatilshay sought an answer, Turtlehead continued. "It is as if someone made medicine against me. Since we began this journey all signs have been bad. Now my arrow misses an easy target. When I reach for you, I fall. I cannot even hit your back with a stone. And see this."

Turtlehead drew his knife from the top of his moccasin. It slid from his fingers and dropped to the ground between them. "I cannot hold a weapon near you."

"You fell on your hand," Hatilshay reminded him.

"That was nothing. It scarcely hurts."

"Many wounds give no pain at first."

"If it is a wound, it is not from a fall." Turtlehead's voice rose. "You always stumble and fall in the dark. Yet when we ran from our sleeping place, it was I who fell. All weapons turn from you, even the rocks. That is why you walk openly to the enemy and speak with him. What medicine do you have that nothing can harm you? And why do you turn it against one of The People?"

"I have no medicine!"

Turtlehead's face showed his disbelief.

"Take your knife in the other hand. Cut me!" Hatilshay held out his arm. Better to risk a serious wound than be whispered a witch and shunned by all The People.

When Turtlehead did not move, Hatilshay stooped

and reached for the knife. An arrow thonked into the dirt beside his hand. Even if it had not pointed from the wrong direction, Hatilshay would have known by the shaft and feathers that it did not come from Turtle-head's bow.

"For a favor, you will let the knife rest." The words were Mexican. The speaker, standing uphill so they were trapped against the boulder, wore white-eye shirt and trousers. But his sandals, headband and face proved what the arrow said . . . Bean People.

2

Witch!

Turtlehead stumbled back against the boulder. "The arrow missed you!"

"It was a warning. He meant it to miss."

"Enemies do not warn."

"You will speak the Mexican," ordered their captor. Then he grinned. "If it is decided that you will live to speak. I do not know if you are worth the killing."

Before Hatilshay could choose between feelings of insult and relief, the young enemy continued. "I come from a long journey to the Yankee towns and have many things to tell my people."

"Go," said Hatilshay. "We do not keep you."

"But you may. That is the difficulty. For the killing of the enemy and the taking of the scalp, there are sixteen days of ceremony."

"That is bad." Hatilshay knew of the Bean People's

foolish belief that a man's spirit remained in the few hairs they took from his lifeless head. He also knew that the days of purification were spent alone, away from the village. "Your tongue is good with stories. One can tell this. Do not make your people wait."

"But there is this to think about. For the scalps of two Apaches, there is still but one ceremony."

"It is said that for two Apaches, one Papago is too little."

"But the one Apache cannot run nor can he hold a knife."

So the Papago was alone. But his words also meant that the first arrow would be Hatilshay's, for Turtlehead could not easily escape. Hatilshay squinted at the fingers on the bow. Their tensing would be his only warning of death. He might dodge the arrow by throwing himself sideways.

"Tell the fool he cannot kill us," said Turtlehead.

"Speak the Mexican," ordered the Papago.

In weak Mexican Turtlehead explained the powers of his blanket and told of Hatilshay's medicine that turned all weapons. It took some time, for Hatilshay refused to help.

The Papago laughed at Turtlehead's blanket, calling it heathen foolishness, but he asked Hatilshay, "Do you wear the medal of a saint? Have you been taught by the priests?"

He must have read the scorn in Hatilshay's face, for he said, "That is very sorry. Now you will go to hell; but that is what one expects for the Apaches."

It was Hatilshay's turn to laugh. "Hell is the place of the Mexicans. Apaches do not go there."

"You will soon know the truth, my friend."

Hatilshay grinned at a wicked idea. Some things The People had in common with enemy tribes.

"Shall I come and tell you the truth, Chulito?"

The Papago's eyes widened. "How did you know my name?"

"I know many things, Chulito. And when I also know about the Mexican hell, I will come back and tell you. I will come at night."

Chulito stepped back and Hatilshay followed. One step, then another.

"I will call and you will hear." Hatilshay flapped his arms like a bird. "Whooooooo! Chulito!"

"Witch!" Turtlehead's voice held as much fear as the Papago's trembling hands.

Hatilshay stalked the enemy, raised his arms and hooted again. A few steps and he could seize the bow. But too late he saw the fingers tighten and knew he'd made a mistake.

Two mistakes. He'd pushed the Papago over the edge of terror and he'd stepped too close to dodge the arrow. Though he knew it was useless, he dropped sideways to the ground. There were thuds, shouts and the world spun.

No, not the world. Just the Papago, jabbed by a cloth-covered hoop on the end of a long stick. Hatilshay sat up to find the arrow had struck the ground only an arm's length beyond his head. The white-eye soldier had turned the Papago's aim. Surely he was one of the friendly soldiers from the Chiricahua Mountains. But how could one be certain? At least one knew what to expect from Mexicans and Bean People.

Hatilshay got to his feet. Head lowered, Chulito listened to the rumbling of the white-eye, answering in that strange tongue.

In their own tongue, Turtlehead asked hoarsely, "How did you know that one's name?"

"The white-eye told me."

"The white-eye said nothing to you. He did not even turn to see you when he motioned. Did you freeze him, witch?"

Turtlehead must be the witch, to have seen all that from where he'd hidden. Luckily, he gave Hatilshay no time to put his thought into words.

"You called the white-eye to you," Turtlehead went on. "You called him with the voice of the spirits."

Hatilshay did not fully believe spirits spoke through the owl. He knew too well that strange and terrible things, when seen closely, were common and harmless as a broken gourd. He suspected the owl was no more to be feared than the roadrunner, which also had strange habits for a bird. But he dared not say this to Turtlehead.

Instead, he answered, "There are some things more to be feared than the voice of an owl, which almost saved us from the Bean People."

"Witch!" Turtlehead whispered.

"A witch would have turned into a coyote and run."

"Not if he has the power to turn away arrows."

"It was the white-eye who turned the arrow."

Turtlehead hugged the end of the folded blanket to his chest. "You claim the white-eye is your medicine. And I heard you call him."

Hatilshay was relieved to have the Papago break the endless circle Turtlehead was talking.

"The captain found your arrow," said Chulito in Mexican. "He followed to speak with you."

"For what?" asked Hatilshay.

"Because he is crazy." The Papago's round face showed that the white-eye soldier's words had not been kind. "All the Yankees are crazy, but this one is more crazy than most. He would speak with the Apache."

The white-eye smiled and held out the lost arrow. Hatilshay gestured toward Turtlehead, who tried to push himself through the boulder. When no one took the arrow, the soldier made his shoulders jump and spoke a few words.

"How many are you?" asked the Papago.

"We are alone."

As the Papago turned his words into the white-eye tongue, the soldier peered up at the shadowed ridge.

"You give the lie!" said Hatilshay and read proof in the Papago's face.

"You do not know the white-eye tongue!"

"I know the Papagos."

"I swear by the Holy Mother . . . ."

The white-eye interrupted. Clearly disapproving, Chulito gave the words to Hatilshay in Mexican.

"The captain says you come to the camp."

"For what?"

Chulito smiled as he had when holding them prisoner.

"The captain kills the bugs and puts them in little boxes. He takes the skins from the animals and these he puts in big boxes. It may be that he has a box for you."

Though Hatilshay did not believe the Papago, the white-eye camp was a danger. But an unknown danger, while death from the Papago was a certainty if they tried to escape. Even if the captain let them go, Chulito would track them next day and Turtlehead could not travel fast enough to take them beyond the Papago's reach.

"We will come," Hatilshay decided. "But I also have a bag. One that will fit a Papago's lying tongue."

He bent and scooped up Turtlehead's knife, grinning as the Papago scurried for the captain's protection. As he slipped the knife into Turtlehead's moccasin the blanket-wearer cringed, but before they were off the slope, he was leaning heavily on Hatilshay's shoulders.

Chulito had difficulty finding a safe trail position. He clearly wished to walk ahead with the captain but did not trust Apaches at his back. Nor would Hatilshay permit the Papago behind theirs. Chulito finally paced far off to one side where he could watch everyone and run in any direction. It angered Hatilshay to think that even his shadow had been mistaken for such a one as the Papago.

Turtlehead stumbled and grew heavier. Hatilshay strained for sight of the white-eye camp. It was strange that Turtlehead had seen no signs. Once they had crossed the ridge, he should have noticed dust from the horses. Then Hatilshay saw the campfires. Shadows had disappeared in the half-light of sunset but there was still light enough to travel a great distance. And the white-eyes were traveling, for Hatilshay counted seven large wagons such as traders used. Among the tents were smaller wagons. Hatilshay could not begin to count the men moving about the camp.

Twice unseen sentries challenged them, earning Hatilshay's respect. Clearly all white-eyes were not as foolish as the captain.

"We wait here." The Papago crouched on his heels before a tent.

The captain ducked under the flap. From inside came a deep voice, growing louder each time the captain spoke.

"What passes?" asked Hatilshay. The Papago looked pleased, so he was sure of hearing the truth.

"The colonel says this is the land of the heathen Apache. The captain must not leave the camp for the Apache devils will kill him. He says it is well known that the Apache have no souls and that they go . . . ."

Hatilshay scowled and the Papago interrupted himself. "The captain says how can he get the bugs and the animals if he does not go out before the wagons chase them away? Now the captain tells that he brings two Apache and the anger of the colonel is magnificent."

The roar from inside the tent proved his words.

Chulito grinned. "The colonel says the Apache must

go, but perhaps he will let you stay when the captain explains that you are for skinning."

Hatilshay did not believe the last but Turtlehead, who understood more Mexican than he spoke, seemed to. He asked help untying the cord around his waist but would not let Hatilshay unfold the blanket. He struggled alone until it was draped over his head and shoulders. With his bent nose and overhung upper lip, he looked like a desert tortoise peering from his shell.

The voices inside the tent lowered. The captain stepped out and spoke to Chulito, who pointed his finger at Turtlehead.

"That one goes with the captain."

"No!" said Turtlehead.

"For what?" Hatilshay asked. "Give me the truth or one Papago will be put in the nest of hungry ants. This I swear."

"The Yankees will not permit this," said Chulito.

"Not while they are here, but the Yankees are few and do not stay. The Apache is always here."

The Papago did not take long to decide. "The captain is one with the medicine. A doctor."

That explained why the colonel feared for his safety. A powerful medicine man was a greater loss than a war leader and the captain must have great power to wander alone with only the hooped stick for a weapon. Hatilshay also believed Chulito when he said the captain wished to heal Turtlehead's leg.

"Such a thing is without reason," said Turtlehead.

"Your uncle has often said the white-eyes are beyond

understanding," Hatilshay reminded him. "It is said they heal enemies they themselves have wounded."

The blanket did not even twitch. Hatilshay knew only one sort of argument would convince Turtlehead and he'd had long practice in using half-truths to avoid lying.

"Did you see a hawk circle the camp?" Hatilshay knew the hawk held great meaning for Turtlehead.

"Did it circle four times?" The head thrust forward to peer from the blanket.

Hatilshay looked at the sky. "I do not see it now."

Turtlehead took the answer as favorable for he rose and held out his right hand to the captain.

"He fell on it," Hatilshay explained to the Papago, acting out the way in which Turtlehead had fallen. The captain did not wait for Chulito's words but spoke rapidly and gestured to another tent.

"The captain will put sticks and bandage on it," said Chulito in Mexican.

"Prayer sticks," said Turtlehead in their own tongue.

He looked pleased with himself as he followed the white-eye captain. Hatilshay was puzzled until he remembered that a witch's medicine could sometimes be used against him. Turtlehead believed he was using white-eye medicine against Hatilshay, who had claimed white-eyes were part of his own medicine. Turtlehead's witch trail was getting harder to untangle. Hatilshay wondered if he'd be permitted to live in camp after Turtlehead told his story. One thing he knew—he was not wanted in the captain's tent.

Chulito carried water pails from a small fire to the medicine tent. He sang as he walked and the words came clearly to Hatilshay, as the Papago meant them to.

"Over the sandy hill they come,
Over the top they come running.
The Apache slave will be killed
And his hide tanned for leather."

Hatilshay thought it a poor war song made worse by turning it into Mexican. Still, it made him uneasy, especially when white-eye soldiers gathered around him. He set his face in the blank mask one showed to strangers.

The white-eyes stared, laughed and whispered just as The People did when a visitor arrived in camp. But this was no friendly camp of The People. These faces were savage and fearful. The pale eyes sent shivers up Hatilshay's spine. Some faces had tails of hair hanging over the lips or were half covered with hair. These white-eyes had the look of animals. And the smell. Hatilshay turned his nose downwind. The white-eyes circled to peer at his face. They moved closer.

Where was Chulito? Without him, Hatilshay could not speak to these savages. Forcing his head to move slowly, he looked around. Chulito was gone and white-eyes surrounded him. Hatilshay tensed, fighting his panic. Then shouts, a crash and yells came from the captain's tent.

White-Eye Witchcraft

Like a pack of dogs, the soldiers ran for the tent opening, pushing to be the first to view what could be their deaths. Truly white-eyes were beyond understanding.

Hatilshay stood and walked around the side of the tent. Once that day he'd walked openly into danger. Because he'd lived to walk away was no reason to risk his life a second time.

Light inside the tent threw shadows on the walls. They moved and disappeared so quickly that Hatilshay did not know if they were made by two persons or three. Listening carefully, he sorted the gabble into three tongues. Two of them he knew but neither made sense.

In his fear, Hatilshay almost called Turtlehead by name. Not his true name, for that Hatilshay did not know. But even an everyday calling name was not used by The People unless there was no other way to name a person. Hatilshay had several ways to call Turtlehead. Before he could use any, the shaman's nephew called him.

"Hatilshay! Come talk for me!"

Though it was only his calling name, its use by the shaman's nephew frightened Hatilshay more than any songs or threats of the Papago's. Had Chulito spoken truth when he talked of skinning? But no, Turtlehead's voice was more outraged than fearful. Certainly he was not in pain.

"I am here," Hatilshay answered. He drew his knife.

"Do not cut the tent," warned Chulito.

Hatilshay glanced around, wondering if the Papago had eyes outside the tent. Then he realized Chulito had only shown more shrewdness than one expected from a Papago. Perhaps he'd learned it from the white-eyes.

Hatilshay walked to the front of the tent. Pushing through those stinking, hairy bodies was worse than any war party could ever be. At last he stood inside the tent, blinking at the strange and wonderful things before him. He was both curious and frightened. When the Papago grinned, Hatilshay knew his face mask had slipped and his feelings showed. Quickly he reset his muscles and kept his eyes only on what was before him.

Tables and raised seats he had heard of, for some Mexicans used them. But Hatilshay had expected them to be larger and heavier. Certainly he had never heard of them opening and closing as did the seat Chulito set out for him.

Turtlehead did not wait for him to sit before commanding, "Tell your white-eye shaman that I am not a piece of deerskin. It is my leg that is torn, not my moccasin."

An open black box filled with strange tools, bottles and pads of cloth was on the table by the white-eye shaman. Beside it was a pan with tiny metal needles, curved like the spine of a barrel cactus. Could the captain truly sew Turtlehead together like a torn moccasin? It would be a wondrous thing to watch and Hatilshay did his best to persuade Turtlehead.

The argument passed through three tongues, losing much in each change and giving Hatilshay time to wonder at the plants, animals and insects spread before him on the table. They must have come from the cloth packs beside them, the same packs the captain had carried. Hatilshay hid his smile. The ground squirrel wasn't there.

"No sewing," Turtlehead said for the fourth time. Without waiting for the words to be given Chulito in Mexican, he added, "Is this part of your witchcraft, to have white-eye magic symbols stitched on my skin?"

Hatilshay gave up arguing. He pushed aside the pan with the needles and said firmly, "No." He made motions of bandaging his own knee.

Through Chulito, the captain said, "It will take longer to heal without the sewing. And it may not heal as well."

"No sewing," said Hatilshay, then kept very still for fear Turtlehead would order him to leave. Without turning his head, he watched a soldier enter the tent, sit down at the opposite side of the table and place a white board near the animals. He began to inspect three dead mice.

Hatilshay asked, "Do the Yankees catch squirrels and mice to get hair to glue on their faces?"

The man poking the mice had thick tufts of hair below his ears, like the whiskers on a bobcat.

"Yankees grow hair on the face, stupid one." Chulito must have seen his glance at the one winding cloth around Turtlehead's knee. He added, "The captain cuts the hair from his face each day with a long knife."

Feeling his own bare chin, Hatilshay tried to imagine thick hair bristling from it. No man of The People had more than a few chin hairs, easily plucked with tin tweezers. Some Mexicans had face hair but it was nothing like the thick mats these white-eyes grew.

"Hair also grows on their chests and under the arms," the Papago told him.

"And the women?"

Chulito's shoulders jumped in the Yankee way. "Is the she-coyote without fur?"

Hatilshay could not hide his disgust. Surely the white-eyes were not real people. He was half convinced they were witches, for the light inside the tent came from three burning sticks, but sticks such as Hatilshay had never seen before. They were pale as a sycamore trunk and the flame at the top did not eat them as fast as flames ate sticks. Also, dribbles like pale honey ran down the sides of the sticks. The drops hardened on Hatilshay's finger and had little taste. The flame burned his finger like true fire, though.

Bobcat Whiskers had been talking with Chulito, who grinned, picked up something from the table and walked around to Hatilshay's side.

"A magic glass," said the Papago, handing Hatilshay a thick round glass on a handle.

Hatilshay held it to his face.

"No, stupid one." Chulito pushed his hand down toward the table.

Hatilshay leaned over but saw only a green bug with thin green wings. He moved his hand away and the bug grew! He looked under the glass. The bug was the proper size. He felt the bottom of the magic glass but it was smooth. Again he watched the bug swell through the glass until it blurred like things in a distance. Hatilshay turned the glass over. Still the bug grew and blurred. In wonder he moved the strange glass over the table, finding pits and craters that were scarcely seen without the glass. Chulito pushed a plant toward him and the magic glass showed the smooth leaf was hairy and the silvery hairs dusty.

He raised the glass and peered through it at Bobcat Whiskers. He saw nothing. Slowly he moved it away from his face and toward the white-eye. The face and tufts of dark whiskers came into view, though not larger than life. As the glass moved farther from Hatilshay's eyes, the white-eye's face blurred, then leaped back *upside down*.

"Yi-i-i!" Hatilshay dropped, then caught, the magic glass.

Bobcat Whiskers stared at him . . . right side up. Hatilshay experimented with the glass until he proved that only in the glass did the white-eye turn head down. And always after a mysterious blurring. He turned and moved the glass toward Turtlehead.

"Witch!" Turtlehead jumped away and threw his blanket over his head.

"I wanted only to see you upside down." Hatilshay pleaded, explained and finally placed blame on the white-eye's magic glass before Turtlehead would come from under the blanket and let the captain finish binding prayer sticks to his hand.

Turtlehead looked sideways at Hatilshay. "Your eye came at me, huge and evil. Do not do that again."

"Not to you," Hatilshay promised. "But perhaps it can be used against enemies. I would like your uncle to see it."

He tried to catch the Papago through it but Chulito stood, back to Hatilshay, watching Bobcat Whiskers working on a white board near the magic flame. The captain finished the bandage and waved Turtlehead out of the tent. The shaman's nephew chose to leave by passing behind Bobcat Whiskers.

He truly thinks me a witch, Hatilshay thought sadly. Then he started at Turtlehead's cry.

"Evil! It is evil!" Forgetting the heavy bandage, Turtlehead tried to claw at Bobcat Whisker's work with his right hand. By the time he freed his other hand from the blanket, Bobcat Whiskers had taken refuge behind the captain. Both white-eyes shouted at each other and Chulito, who shouted back and grinned. Hatilshay understood only Turtlehead. At least, he understood the words, though not their meaning.

"He caught your life spirit," Turtlehead told him. "Your life spirit is there, on that thing. He can make medicine against you. He can . . . I do not know what he can do."

His voice held such fear that Hatilshay's legs weakened and cold spread out from his middle. He wished he could understand what the Papago was telling the white-eyes, who looked from Hatilshay to Turtlehead as they listened.

When Chulito stopped talking and the white-eyes began arguing with one another, Hatilshay asked in Mexican, "What lies did you give them?"

"I told them the Apache is a heathen and has no civilizing."

Since Hatilshay did not know if civilizing came from witchcraft or protected one from it, he said only, "You used many words to say little."

"What the Apache does not know takes many words." Chulito listened to the captain, then told Hatilshay, "Go look. You will see it is nothing. He put you on the paper but he puts everything on the paper."

Bobcat Whiskers held out his work and turned the white leaves. Hatilshay moved close and bent to see plants, lizards, spiders and insects, all caught by white-eye magic. Though they seemed to have form, Hatilshay felt only the rough paper before Bobcat Whiskers pushed his fingers away. All had a dead look which did not come just from lack of color. The lizards did not hold their heads as they should and plant leaves spread flat as no leaf did in life. Then Bobcat Whiskers turned the last page and fear such as Hatilshay had never known paralyzed his muscles and voice. The white-eye witch had caught one of The People!

"It is your life spirit," Turtlehead repeated in a whisper. "Take it back."

Trusting Turtlehead in the matter of magic and witches, Hatilshay told Chulito, "I must have that."

"You are an ignorant savage," said the Papago. "I have seen many faces on the walls of Yankee houses. It is an honor they give their great ones."

"And where are the great ones? Did you see them walking in true life?"

Chulito's smug look faded. Quickly he made the magic sign of the black-robed priests. "It is a sin to listen to heathen devils. I am a good Christian."

With his good hand, Turtlehead made a cutting motion across his throat and said in Mexican, "Make good Papago."

The captain's mouth twitched at the corners. Chulito saw, for he'd turned as if to ask protection. Instead, he looked death at Turtlehead. Hatilshay had to repeat his demand twice before the Papago gave some words to the captain. It must have been the truth, for after a short argument with the captain, Bobcat Whiskers tore away the leaf with Hatilshay's spirit on it and held it out. His look, at both Hatilshay and Turtlehead, was as deadly as the Papago's.

"Hide it quickly," Turtlehead advised. After watching Hatilshay fold it and tuck it into his moccasin top, he led the way from the tent.

The time in the tent had seemed long, but the half light that came after sunset still lingered. Behind the ridge the sky was red and orange. Soon the color would fade and though Hatilshay would sit in darkness, light would show above the ridge as if the land beyond still held the day. Hatilshay knew if he crossed the ridge he would find the land beyond just as dark, with the promise of day showing beyond the next ridge.

"Spirit magic," he murmured.

"It must be destroyed," said Turtlehead.

Hatilshay stared at him, then caught his meaning. "I will put it in a fire."

"No!" Turtlehead drew his blanket closer about his shoulders. "If you burn your spirit, will you not burn also?"

Cut it in pieces? Bury it? Everything Hatilshay thought of brought visions of his own unpleasant death. He wasn't certain Turtlehead was right but this was one time he dared not gamble.

"I will ask your uncle," he decided. "The old one will know what to do."

As Turtlehead grunted approval, Chulito strode past. Without looking at them he said, "The captain said I must feed the Apache dogs."

"What did he say?" asked Turtlehead.

Hatilshay's stomach persuaded him to misunderstand. "He said he must feed the Apaches and the dogs."

"There are no dogs in camp."

"Except that one." Hatilshay nodded at the Papago.

They followed Chulito to a cook fire where an old soldier ladled stew onto shallow tin plates. Biscuits were added, then each of them was given a plate and a pair of metal tools. One looked like a long-handled comb but when Hatilshay drew it through his long hair, Chulito and the old soldier laughed. The knife, at least, might be of value if properly sharpened. Hatilshay thrust both into his moccasin.

"You must return the knife and fork to the cook," said Chulito, "or he will name you a thief."

"He gave them to me!"

"They are only for eating. After the eating, you must give them back."

While Hatilshay tried to make sense of his words, Chulito settled cross-legged on the ground with the food pan balanced on his ankles. With the comb tool he speared a chunk of meat and held it to the pan while he cut it into smaller pieces. Then he used the strange tool to carry the small pieces one by one to his mouth. When his cheeks bulged, he chewed and swallowed.

"That is the way of the Papagos?" asked Hatilshay.

"That is the way of the civilized."

"It is the stupid way." Hatilshay hunkered down on his heels. Sitting cross-legged was dangerous. He could not rise quickly if the soldiers attacked. Also, he could see no reason to cut meat that was already a size to fit the mouth. Raising the pan to his chin, he scooped stew into his mouth, then sopped the last of the gravy with the biscuits.

While he sawed at his meat, Chulito boasted of his own importance. "The captain and I ride out each day, in front of all the others. Every plant and animal I name for him, finding one of each for his little boxes. It is work of the greatest importance, for all will be sent back to the schools in the great towns. Also I care for the captain, showing what is harmful, scouting for the devil Apache and guiding the captain back to the wagons."

He must have been scouting in the wrong direction when Hatilshay had walked up to the captain and the ground squirrel. To push aside the thought of what might have happened, Hatilshay asked, "And did the captain hear of your greatness all the way to the Yankee towns? Did he send for the great Chulito to guide him?"

The Papago chewed and swallowed before he could answer. "I was in one of the great towns, in one of the Yankee schools. One other and I were sent to learn the Yankee tongue and the Yankee ways. The other caught the coughing sickness and died." He crossed himself. "God rest his soul."

"Is his spirit picture on a Yankee wall?" asked Hatilshay.

Chulito glanced at him, crossed himself again and muttered a Mexican prayer. Sensing a weakness, Hatilshay jabbed again.

"And then the great and brave Chulito fled before his spirit was captured and placed on the wall."

"That is not the truth." Chulito attacked the meat as if it were an enemy. "The captain came to the school, asking for help. I thought of my people and all the wonders of which I could tell them. It is true that I was to stay longer, but the captain needed help. I said I would go. It has been a slow journey of many months."

Weary of his boasting, Hatilshay asked about the wonders of the Yankee towns. At first he believed the

Papago. The Hopi also built houses of many levels and the great iron beast that breathed smoke and fire was like one in the tales of Child-of-Water, though Hatilshay marveled that the white-eyes had tamed the monster to run on two paths of iron. But when Chulito claimed that one Yankee town held more people than all the villages of the Papago, their cousins and their allies, Hatilshay knew he lied and told him so.

Though the night was chill, Turtlehead and Hatilshay were forced back into the shadows. Instead of a small fire that friends could gather near, the white-eyes had piled on wood as if planning to roast a standing mule. Men moved beyond the fire, harness jingled, a horse snorted.

"They post many sentries," said Turtlehead.

Hatilshay nodded as if he, too, had seen. Chulito came and held out his hand.

"The knife and fork," he demanded. When he had them he added, "Do not think you can steal from this camp. There will be sentries watching you all night. You cannot sneak away in the dark."

Turtlehead nodded and said, "It is true. I cannot slip between the sentries. My wounds make me clumsy."

Even if Hatilshay could bring himself to escape without Turtlehead, he feared he would blunder into a sentry, mistaking him for a sheltering bush.

"And tomorrow?" he asked Chulito. "What then?"

The Papago grinned and drew his hand across his throat. "Maybe make good Apaches."

4

The
Long
Eye

Hatilshay woke to kicks and hisses. Turtlehead bent over him.

"Look what your white-eye shaman has done!"

Too sleepy to protest, Hatilshay let himself be dragged to his feet. The sky was light behind the mountains but he could not see what was wrong with Turtlehead's hand until they bent close to the dying fire. Above the bandage the fingers were purple and swollen larger than if seen through the captain's magic glass. Hatilshay cut away the bandage. The hand at the base of the thumb looked worse than the fingers. Even the wrist was swollen and discolored.

"Does it hurt?" he asked.

"My fingers feel nothing. I cannot move them!"

Turtlehead's left hand fumbled among the bandages

for the flat sticks which strips of cloth had held tight to his thumb and hand. The sticks were also wound in white cloth.

"When your white-eye shaman bound these prayer sticks to my hand, I believed he meant to heal. Now I know they are evil." Turtlehead dropped them on the fire and watched them burn. "My uncle will cure my hand. I must go to him."

"Has your leg healed during the night?"

"I will not need to walk."

Hatilshay shook his head. "They will not let us near the horses. Why do you think they keep us in the center of the camp, with sentries around us?"

"I have listened to the night voices. I have seen omens in the sky. Soon we will have help."

Hatilshay knew that without the aid of omens. Dust from the wagons could be seen for a great distance. Turtlehead would have seen the cloud the day before if the ridge had not been in the way. It had probably been sighted from the mountains long ago. Already scouts must be coming to see who passed and if they could be raided. Since the white-eye camp was large and well guarded, men of The People might not show themselves. But they would follow and perhaps move ahead to leave sign for Turtlehead and Hatilshay to read.

"Leave the bandage on my knee," ordered Turtlehead, though Hatilshay had made no move to cut it. "They must see that I am wounded and do not stay for love of the white-eye."

"Nor do I," said Hatilshay.

Turtlehead did not argue but he smiled as he bent over the charred sticks. Did he search for omens, a cure or the face of a witch? Turtlehead's omens always answered his wishes, yet Hatilshay was certain he did not lie. Perhaps Turtlehead's eyes did not see true either. Hatilshay shook his head. Omens would not help them escape from the white-eye camp.

Usually Hatilshay left ceremonies to others, but as the sun rose he felt a need for comfort. He moved from the campfire toward a small rise where he could be alone. He'd gone only ten paces when an armed soldier rose from behind a bush. Hatilshay turned back. Before reaching the fire, he drew hoddentin from the pouch at his waist and offered the pollen to the four directions. Then he settled to wait for Turtlehead to finish.

The shaman's nephew chanted softly to east, south, west and north. His prayers were so long that Hatilshay thought the gods must weary of him. Before he finished, the soldiers had roused and come to stare.

Horses were saddled, the guards changed. The medicine tent was taken down and packed in a small wagon. Still they sat, though sensible travelers would have been on the trail long before.

Chulito hurried up, full of his own importance. He pointed a finger at Turtlehead instead of motioning the proper way with his chin. "That one cannot walk. You will ride in the captain's wagon."

"He can sit a horse," Hatilshay told him.

"The Apache is not to be trusted with the horses. You will ride in the wagon. And do not think to make trouble. You will be watched."

Then he left, walking stiff like a white-eye. Hatilshay helped Turtlehead into the wagon, then sat beside him among bundles and wooden boxes. There was much noise and confusion by the trade wagons. Whips popped, sounding so much like gunshots that Hatilshay jumped. The wagons moved forward in two lines. A soldier climbed to the high driver's seat and the captain's wagon lurched and joggled ahead.

Dust swirled over them. Turtlehead pulled his blanket closer but Hatilshay could only crouch with arms over his head. He knew from creaks and jangling on either side that they moved between the two rows of heavy trade wagons. The dust lessened and he raised his head. The captain's light wagon had moved to the front and led the way. No, mounted soldiers led and many more rode guard to the sides and far back in the dust. No scout of The People would get close enough to see who lay in the wagon. There would be no message stones placed on the trail ahead.

Turtlehead grumbled from his blanket, "I have walked faster than this."

"You could not today," Hatilshay reminded him. "And we move in the right direction."

They might still find a way to escape. And slow travel gave Turtlehead's leg a chance to heal. Once more on the move, with the sun warming his back, Hatilshay felt more hopeful.

The captain rode his horse up beside the wagon, holding out bean pods and asking by signs if he could eat them. Hatilshay nodded and watched with amusement as the captain sampled the beans. Pods still on paloverdes at this season were hard enough to hurt teeth. The captain frowned and rode off. Hatilshay wondered if he knew to grind them between stones.

The white-eye shaman returned with empty yucca pods and mesquite beans. Behind him came Chulito, scowling and making his horse move side to side as if impatient to race. Because it angered the Papago, Hatilshay nodded yes or no to each plant the captain brought him. It puzzled the white-eye to receive both answers to a mescal leaf but by then Hatilshay had wearied of the game. He put his head down on his folded arms and pretended to sleep. Let the Papago explain, if he could, that it was not the leaf one ate.

They soon stopped to rest the horses, though they'd gone hardly any distance. Before they moved on, the captain moved boxes and bundles so he could sit in the wagon opposite Hatilshay and Turtlehead. Chulito tied their horses to the wagon and climbed in beside the captain, grumbling and complaining about having to speak for the Apache devils.

"I want no more of your white-eye's healing," Turtlehead warned Hatilshay.

"Speak the Mexican," said Chulito.

Hatilshay eyed the horses, bobbing along behind the wagon. They could not take them and race through the white-eye guards, not even if Turtlehead had full use of his leg. But it was torture having them almost in arm's reach.

Chulito's surly voice broke into his thoughts. "The captain wants friend in the Apache."

Hatilshay pretended not to understand. "I am no enemy to the captain."

While Chulito explained that the captain wanted the Apache word for friend. Hatilshay tried to decide if he should answer. None of The People would believe a Papago who said he was a friend. But one could not be certain about white-eyes. Some of The People might believe and the white-eye could be an enemy in waiting. In the end, it was the Papago who decided him. Chulito began looking pleased with the lengthening silence.

Hatilshay gave the word, watching Chulito's face closely. The captain repeated it incorrectly.

"Witch!" said Turtlehead, but he did not mean Hatilshay. "They are all witches, these white-eyes!"

The captain used tools like Bobcat Whiskers'. Hatilshay scrambled over bundles to pull the small white square from the captain's hand. He had time only to see that the marks formed nothing he knew before Chulito snatched it back.

"What is that?" demanded Hatilshay.

"It is your word, stupid one. The captain puts it on the paper and all the Yankees can hear it. Then all can speak with the Apache. I have told him they will learn nothing."

"It is true." Turtlehead's voice was muffled by the

red blanket. If he heard Chulito's order to speak the Mexican, he did not heed it. "My uncle has said that the Mexicans also have these talking signs. They must be evil. Do not give the white-eye any of our words."

Hatilshay also ignored Chulito, who looked thunderous. "Can the white-eye catch the spirit of a word?"

"Would you give him your name?"

"No!" For a short space Hatilshay was too shocked to think. Then he said slowly, "My name is breath and blood of my spirit. Those who use it have power over me, but what power can they have over a word?"

"Anything can be turned to evil. Give them nothing."

He was right. Hatilshay kept silent. Chulito and the white-eye shaman traded words. Neither looked pleased.

At last Chulito spoke in Mexican. "The captain wishes only to be friend to the Apache. To be a friend, he must know the Apache tongue."

"To be a friend, he can let us go."

"Go!" Chulito waved at the mountains. "No one is keeping you."

"A trap," muttered Turtlehead.

Hatilshay agreed. The Papago was too eager and he remembered well the guard he'd almost stumbled over that morning only a few steps from the campfire.

Hatilshay motioned to the red and yellow bundle beside him. "That one cannot walk. We stay."

Chulito looked angrier than ever. He and the captain talked while the wagon lurched and jolted. They'd come almost as far since the rest stop as they had before it. On foot, Hatilshay could have traveled the whole distance three times and the sun would be no higher.

The Papago looked at Hatilshay and grinned. "The captain wants your name."

The blanket-wearer growled. Fear crawled up Hatilshay's chest, then turned to anger. Chulito knew, if the captain did not, that The People seldom gave true names even to each other. To a stranger, they would not give even an ordinary calling name.

Hatilshay said, "Say to the captain I cannot give it."

"It is a superstition of the heathen and he will not understand."

"Did you give him your name?"

Chulito's eyes narrowed. "He speaks it."

It was the sort of answer Hatilshay often gave. Chulito was certainly not the Papago's true name. It was probably not even the calling name used by his people but one given by the Mexicans, who lived in walled towns near the Papago.

"Would the captain give me his name?" asked Hatilshay.

"The Yankees give their names to everyone. It means nothing."

"You give me the lie."

"I speak the truth. He will give you his name."

Turtlehead poked his nose from the blanket. "Take it!"

"It may be a trap," Hatilshay told him.

The captain pointed his writing tool at his chest and

spoke something like *capitán,* with half the sounds left out. He then pointed at Chulito, said the Papago's name and pointed in silence at Hatilshay. Before Hatilshay could decide what to say, the wagon stopped.

"We eat now," said Chulito.

Turtlehead needed help to climb from the wagon. Though his face showed nothing, Hatilshay felt his arm muscles tense with pain as he moved his wounded leg. The unbandaged arm he kept hidden beneath the blanket. When the captain brought the black box of tools, he refused to let the leg bandage be touched.

"But it is worse than it was," Hatilshay told him.

"It is worse because the white-eye witches are near. The other one, the Bobcat Whiskers, rode near us. Always he watched. He was working magic against me." He drew deeper into his blanket. "The evil one comes."

Bobcat Whiskers bent to look at a box fastened under the wagon, then made marks on the white pad he carried. The box was at the wheel, near where Turtlehead had sat.

"What is that?" Hatilshay asked Chulito.

"It counts the turns of the wheel to give the length of the journey."

Hatilshay turned his back and went to sit beside Turtlehead. As if he didn't know that the number of days gave the length of the journey. To hide his anger, he asked the blanket-wearer, "How is the hand?"

"It aches. Not much, but it will be worse. The omens are all bad."

"I have seen nothing."

"Why should you? You are friend to the white-eye witches. It is I they work against."

His tone hinted that Hatilshay worked with them. Hatilshay glanced around, for no one had told them to speak the Mexican.

"Where is the Papago?" The horses were gone from the back of the wagon. "And the horses?"

"The Papago went with the evil one, leading the horses. Perhaps they have gone."

More likely Chulito had taken the horses to graze. Cook fires had been built, though the team had not been freed from the captain's wagon. The white-eyes had made camp just to eat. Perhaps they did count the turns of the wheel. One thing was no more foolish than the other.

Three soldiers came to the captain for cures. Two received charms from the black box. The other rolled back his sleeve. Chulito had not lied about the hair. It lay thick and black on the white-eye's arm. The captain climbed into the wagon and rummaged in a bundle, returning with the magic glass. He crouched over the soldier's arm, working with tweezers. After a while, the captain glanced over at Hatilshay, smiled and motioned him to come look.

He was not removing hair, as Hatilshay had thought, He was pulling out cactus spines, the kind one had to leave in until they festered because they couldn't be seen. Under the magic glass, they were large as fine hairs. Full of excitement, Hatilshay returned to Turtlehead's side.

"That magic glass is a wondrous thing," he told him.

"For witches," said Turtlehead, and drew himself deeper into the medicine blanket.

When finished with the soldier, the captain tried to press the magic glass into Hatilshay's hand. Hatilshay refused, for he felt Turtlehead stiffen in fear or disapproval. If they escaped from the white-eyes, they would live among The People. Hatilshay did not want Turtlehead naming him witch, not for so small a thing as looking at a pebble through the magic glass. He was glad he'd looked through it the night before.

"Chulito!" The captain looked around, frowning and calling the Papago's name. He stared at Hatilshay as if deciding on a cure, then put the magic glass and black box in the back of the wagon. He raised his hand in salute and left.

Meat and biscuits were cooked and eaten. Hatilshay gulped the hot dark liquid he'd been given. Sugar dug from the bottom of the tin cup chased the bitterness from his mouth. Still the white-eyes lounged beside the fires.

The captain returned, crouched beside Hatilshay and handed him a thick black reed with circles of glass closing each end. Hatilshay shook it but could hear nothing, though it hefted as if something was inside. The captain smiled and pointed from the small end to his right eye.

Another magic glass! Turtlehead murmured from inside his blanket. Hatilshay held the reed toward the captain, who waved his hand and spoke rapidly, pointing from the reed to his eye to the mountains.

"It is evil," warned Turtlehead.

"The glass is smaller so its power must be less." But there were two glasses on the reed, which only strengthened Hatilshay's curiosity. "We must discover their magic and tell your uncle."

Without waiting for an answer, Hatilshay raised the reed to his eye. A bush thirty steps away leaped close as his nose. Instead of blurred masses, the waxy leaves were clear and separate.

"It is a long eye," Hatilshay cried.

In wonder he turned, looking through the reed. The mountains came close as if he and Turtlehead had pushed hard all day. He could see clearly the hairy faces of the men scuffing dirt on the farthest cook fire. The large cloth-covered wagons at the far side of the camp came near as the captain's wagon. The drivers did not wear the blue uniforms nor did they camp with the soldiers. They must be different, as the Papagos and Hopis were different. Did that make them more peaceful or less trustworthy than the soldiers?

As he swung the long eye in a slow arc, he saw drivers checking harness and climbing to seats. They must be ready to move at last. Someone dropped from a blue covered wagon and reached up to receive a large flat box. It was Chulito! Hatilshay stared as Bobcat Whiskers climbed from the back of the wagon and took the box from Chulito. The Papago drew the edge of his hand across his throat and they both laughed.

The captain's hand tugged gently at the long eye.

With a sigh, Hatilshay released it. Not since his first bow and arrows had he yearned for anything as he did for this long eye. He had seen the world as the hawk must, circling beyond sight. Now he saw only a short way before him, like an ant. Ant Eyes they should call him, not Hatilshay, the name of people who lived far to the west and dreamed even when awake. Turtlehead's uncle had given him the name, for the shaman had once visited those people. Hatilshay wondered if the name had been a joke, if the shaman had always known what Hatilshay did now. But how could the old one have known how little Hatilshay saw? Without the long eye, Hatilshay would not have begun to suspect what others saw.

The captain had been speaking for some time. He pointed the long eye at the mountains.

"Yes," said Hatilshay, but when he reached for the long eye it was jerked from his hand. He at last understood that the captain wanted something. When he'd received it, Hatilshay could again look through the long eye. Or perhaps he would be given it. Truly it was a great gift, but white-eyes might scatter long eyes as freely as The People did hoddentin. Who could say?

Again the captain pointed to the mountains. Hatilshay closed his ears to anything Turtlehead might say and answered, "Home."

The white-eye pointed west.

"Papago land," said Hatilshay.

The captain looked displeased and began again with the mountains of home.

"I do not understand," said Hatilshay. He repeated it in Mexican.

"Chulito!" roared the captain.

The Papago hurried up, grinning and casting sly looks at Hatilshay and Turtlehead. Whatever the captain wanted, it had to wait until they had all climbed back into the wagon. Riding there took away some of Chulito's joy. When they had jogged and bounced to the front of the wagon line, the Papago made a great show of brushing the dust from his shirt and pants.

"The captain wants the word for mountain," he said.

Turtlehead warned, "He will paint the words."

Hatilshay repeated it in Mexican.

"But yes!" Chulito wore his superior look. "The civilized write everything. I myself can write some. Only the ignorant savage fears it."

A thought had been growing in Hatilshay's mind. He released it. "Will the captain write his name and give it to me?"

There was a sound of approval from the blanket.

"Heathen superstition," said Chulito, but he turned the words into the captain's tongue. The white-eye shaman spoke his name, pointing to himself. To Hatilshay's ears it was harsh. Then he drew whirls and lines that had no design and gave the square to Hatilshay. Either it was not the captain's name or Turtlehead was wrong about writing having power over things. Just to be certain, Hatilshay returned the white square.

"Have him write the name of the long eye," Hatilshay told the Papago.

If Turtlehead was right, the long eye might be his soon. He need only learn how to use the writing to draw it to him.

"Get the Papago's name," said Turtlehead.

"No, for we cannot know what he tells the white-eye to write."

"Then you may have power over nothing."

"Perhaps." But there was need to speak to the white-eyes without the Papago. Also, Hatilshay wished to look once more through the long eye. How many words before the captain would let him?

He answered most of the questions despite Turtle-head's mumbled warnings and prayers. If the drawings were no better than the captain's pronunciation, the blanket-wearer had nothing to fear. Hatilshay had given only ten or so words when a soldier ran up and stopped the wagon.

"Do we eat again?" asked Hatilshay.

Chulito shook his head. "A wagon needs repair. It is time to rest the horses anyway. The stop will only be a little longer."

Hatilshay rose stiffly. Walking was not only faster, it did not leave one bruised and full of splinters. He thought he would have to lift Turtlehead from the wagon. He staggered and almost fell under the weight.

"My leg will not bend," Turtlehead complained. "Am I turning to stone like the warriors in the old tales?"

"I am stiff also," Hatilshay told him.

"But you walk easier with each step. I do not." He shuffled away from the wagon. "I will not walk easy until my uncle sings over me."

Chulito said softly, "Tell the other one I have something to show him."

"You tell him." Hatilshay was waiting for the captain to bring him the long eye.

"He will not hear if I tell him. Say it is the work of the one who paints the pictures."

Bobcat Whiskers couldn't have caught Turtlehead's spirit. The shaman's nephew hadn't put his head outside the blanket since he'd learned of the danger. But Chulito's smile made Hatilshay fearful. He told Turtlehead what Chulito had said.

"I will go," he said, and hobbled behind the Papago, leaning on Hatilshay's arm.

They only had to walk to the third wagon, one with a blue covering. Hatilshay boosted the blanket-wearer up to the back. He had to balance sideways on a ledge only half as wide as his foot. Hatilshay climbed up to steady him and see what was inside. He pulled back the heavy cloth so they could peer in. Light filtered through the cloth was so dim that Hatilshay at first saw only long wrapped bundles. Then he saw that the cloth wrapping had been taken from one. It was more than one of Bobcat Whiskers' dead pictures; it was the image of a full-size man, lying almost face down. Hatilshay scarcely noticed the head or black hair. There was no need, for there was no mistaking the red and yellow blanket covering the back of the figure.

Turtlehead yelled and lost his balance. Hatilshay jumped and kept him from falling on the ground.

"I am turned to stone," moaned Turtlehead.

When Hatilshay said as much to Chulito, the Papago said, "Not stone. Wood. He now belongs to the Yankees."

Turtlehead trembled so that he could hardly stand. "I am turning to wood. I can feel the stiffness growing. Soon my spirit will walk the night."

Hatilshay urged him back to the wagon but he refused to go.

"I will sit here," he said. "I go no farther with the white-eye witches."

Since he thought himself dying, he didn't care that a sentry might shoot him. But Hatilshay wasn't longing for a bullet.

Softly, Chulito sang,

> "Yankee magic shapes the world.
>   See what it can do?
>   Into wood the Yankee turns him.
>   See what he can do!"

Hatilshay turned on him. "The Apache knife shapes the Papago tongue. Would you see what it can do?"

Chulito danced away. When the captain came to speak, the Papago was not with him. The white-eye pointed toward the mountains of home. Hatilshay hoped it meant the sentries would ride past them without threat. When Hatilshay said friend in his own tongue, the captain nodded and repeated it better than he had before. A short while later, the wagons rolled past. A few soldiers glanced down at them as they rode by. Chulito passed, leading the captain's horse and singing loudly of Yankee magic. When the dust had settled, Turtlehead drew the blanket from his face to speak with Hatilshay.

"You have done this. It was you who saw the white-eye in the vision and sent us down the hillside."

Hatilshay wanted to deny seeing a vision. That was something even shamans rarely did. Turtlehead gave him no chance.

"You approached the white-eye," he continued. "You called him with the voice of the spirits and sent me to his medicine tent. Do not think that I will forget."

Hatilshay said only, "We will leave blame for your uncle to decide. Come."

"It is too late."

"Not if we can reach your uncle. Come, the Papago may circle back." When Turtlehead stirred nervously, he added, "He may bring the white-eye witch."

That got Turtlehead to his feet. His legs were as stiff as he had claimed, but by threats of white-eye magic and hope of the shaman's cure Hatilshay kept him moving. When all else failed, he half carried the sweating blanket-wearer. Though panting and weakening, Turtlehead kept reminding him of things he would not forget until Hatilshay wished the stiffening had begun with his tongue. Especially when they met three scouts of The People.

Turtlehead did not name him witch but his story put the fear in the men. Hatilshay read it in the way they avoided him and fell silent when he approached. If this was his treatment from men of a different village, what would life in his own be like? Would his people tire of the witch fear and drive him out? It had happened before. The Navajo were said to come from a witch driven out by The People.

One of the scouts had been cured of antelope sickness by Turtlehead's uncle. He hurried to summon the old one, for Turtlehead's leg was bleeding again and Hatilshay could not drag him much farther. Their days became an uneven pattern of short journeys, each only as long as Turtlehead's strength. Hatilshay used the long rests to test Bobcat Whiskers' spirit picture.

Where the square folded, the marks had blurred. After careful thought, Hatilshay rubbed the chin to a gray smudge. He spent a fitful night, waking often to feel his jaw. One by one he rubbed away the features until the picture looked like a storm cloud. Then he struck spark to dry grass, crumpled the square and fed it to the tiny flame.

Did he live because he'd defeated the white-eye magic or because there had been nothing to fear? And why didn't the captain's talking signs smear also? If the marks were stronger, surely the magic must be too, yet the long eye still journeyed with the white-eye soldiers. Hatilshay puzzled the questions while they struggled into the foothills, where the old one found them.

5

The
Old
One

"My nephew has spoken of a spirit picture." The shaman had spent most of a day and night treating Turtlehead's wounds with herbs and his stiffness with chanting. Yet he looked no more weary than when he'd slid from his horse. His face was lined but when he offered sacred pollen to the rising sun and returned to Turtlehead's side, his step was firm and his back straight.

Sometime during the cure Turtlehead must have told his story. Hatilshay had not heard it. He'd crept about on guard. Not that he trusted his eyes enough to see an enemy, but he'd had no wish to hear himself named witch. Not to the old one, who was closer to Hatilshay than his own grandfather. Now, crouched opposite the shaman with Turtlehead stretched between them, Hatilshay waited for the shaman's anger.

"I do not have the spirit picture."

Turtlehead struggled to sit up. "You lost it? Left it for someone to find?"

"No."

"He destroyed it." The shaman's narrow eyes watched Hatilshay like a roadrunner waiting to race, as if he knew beforehand which way Hatilshay would run. Hatilshay had often squirmed beneath that look when the old one had taught him to speak Mexican or answered questions about his travels as a young man.

"How could he destroy it and remain unharmed?" Turtlehead might as well have added, Unless he is a witch, for the words hung between them as if spoken.

"I found a way." Hatilshay wished they would stop speaking of him as if he wasn't there. Or was that the way one spoke in front of witches?

"Then a way can be found to destroy the spirit carving," said the shaman. "Perhaps the same way can be used."

"We must take him with us." Again Turtlehead spoke as if Hatilshay had turned to smoke and blown away.

Perhaps his own eyes and ears were playing false. A thumbnail dug into his leg proved to Hatilshay that he was solid and very much present. To prove it to Turtlehead he said, "I do not wish to go."

He straightened and walked to a rock overlooking a narrow riverbed. The shaman's light step followed. Hatilshay waited but did not turn.

The shaman spoke slowly, as if choosing each word with the care of a hunter selecting arrows. "My nephew has a great fear of the white-eye's carving. It is making a cripple of him. It may be that he will think to loose the spirit from his body."

How could Turtlehead have a choice about his death if the spirit carving caused the stiffness? Or had the shaman meant that Turtlehead's fear was causing it? The order of his words gave two meanings.

"I take my nephew to see the carving destroyed. He believes you have great power with the white-eyes. Will you travel with us?"

"Your nephew believes I am a witch."

"Do you believe you are a witch?"

Hatilshay turned, expecting to meet the sly road-runner look, but the old man's eyes were serious, as if listening to a sick man. Not knowing what cure might follow, Hatilshay feared to give any answer without more thought. Movement in the bushes near the river-bed caught his attention. Without a second look he changed the path of their words. "We need meat."

"Not as much as my nephew needs the horse to ride."

Too late Hatilshay noticed the size of the animal and the clumsiness that could only be from hobbles. He glanced at the wrinkled face but found no sign of amusement.

"I will get the horse." Hatilshay scrambled down the rocky slope to the riverbed. The animal was old and bent, fit only for the cook pot. Perhaps the shaman had not guessed his mistake in thinking it a deer, but Hatilshay wondered again if the old one knew of his untruthful vision. It was the shaman who'd given him his calling name, the name of men to the west by the great river who dreamed while awake. Yet the shaman himself did that. His eyes were narrow and wrinkled at the corners from much staring into the far distance. At what, no one could say.

As he waited for the horse to drink, Hatilshay worried over the shaman's question. He did not believe himself a witch but that did not mean he wasn't. A rabbit could believe himself a coyote but would be a rabbit all the same. Until his false belief put him in reach of a real coyote's jaw.

Hatilshay slapped the horse's rump, chasing it up the bank. Perhaps he should stay away from The People. The scouts who had heard Turtlehead's story would surely repeat it. The one who had summoned the old one would have told it in Hatilshay's own village. Life there, for a time, might become uneasy.

Then, too, if the old one followed the soldiers, Hatilshay might have a chance to look again through the long eye. Perhaps the talking signs he carried in his moccasin had all the power Turtlehead claimed, but Hatilshay did not know how to use them. Or perhaps they had no power at all.

When he'd slung the shaman's buckskin food pouches over the horse's flanks and helped Turtlehead to its back, Hatilshay strung his bow and followed the old one.

Turtlehead looked down at him. "You said that you did not want to travel with us."

"Your uncle's words changed my wishes."

"It is my thought you want only to see the white-eye shaman again."

The words were too near the truth. Hatilshay moved off to one side, too far for Turtlehead's words to reach him yet close enough to keep sight of the horse. By the time he realized the horse had stopped and had circled back to find the reason, the shaman had finished council with the scout. He was the same man who'd summoned the shaman. The old one took something from the pouch at his waist and gave it to the scout, who disappeared like a lizard into the desert.

"The white-eyes did not stop," Turtlehead called down to Hatilshay. "They have gone toward the setting sun and the big river."

"The wagons travel slowly," Hatilshay reminded him.

"Dust spirits have crossed their trail."

The huge whirling dust storms would cover all trace of wagons and horses. Before Turtlehead could accuse him of calling up wind and sand, Hatilshay said, "Perhaps the white-eye witch called on the dust spirits for help."

"Whoever called them, the trail is gone," said the shaman. His eyes glimmered as Turtlehead pulled the red blanket over his head. "We must learn where the white-eyes have taken the spirit carving."

"Is there a ceremony that will tell us?" Hatilshay knew there was but dared not ask directly if Turtlehead's uncle had that power.

The smile in the old one's eyes reached his lips. "There is a Papago who will tell us."

Remembering the scout, Hatilshay did not have to ask Turtlehead how they would find Chulito. What he wished to know, he feared to ask. Certainly Turtle-head, his legs stiff as lances on each side of the horse, could not steal Chulito from an enemy village. Perhaps the shaman had a ceremony to draw the Papago to him. Hatilshay believed that during the day but at night his doubts grew. Hatilshay knew he could creep into a Papago village easily enough but he feared he would never get out.

He would tell the old one he was returning to the winter camp. But each morning he met the wise road-runner look and could not force the words past his tongue. He decided to leave without speaking but the days passed without the proper time being found. When the shaman left Turtlehead and the horse hidden among red rocks and crawled through the dusk to the fields of a Papago village, Hatilshay squirmed on his belly beside him.

6

Chulito
Again

Hatilshay raised his head and sniffed. Horses! The shaman must know of them. He'd spent much of the day
watching this village. Did the old one plan to stampede
the herd and escape on horseback? Horses would be of
more use than Chulito, though they would have to take
the Papago too.

Dried cotton stalks, hard as arrow shafts, jabbed
Hatilshay's side. They did not break the skin but left
painful bruises. Carefully he crept to the edge of the
field. The village had few of the round brush huts,
much like wickiups, that Papagos usually built. Most
of the dark shapes rose as square and unnatural as the
church towering over them. Papagos seldom wandered
far from their rivers and fields but these must never
move at all.

"Wait here," whispered the shaman. "When I signal,
come with empty hands." He slid noiselessly over the

dirt ridge marking the end of the field and disappeared.

Hatilshay's unstrung bow was already in its case. Any enemy he saw at night would be close enough for his knife. He eased it from his moccasin and tried not to hear the field noises. Every mouse rustle became a sneaking Papago. A stem against his neck was a hand. He shivered and tried to keep his thoughts on the signal. That was worry enough.

How was he to see it when he could no longer find the old one among the shadows? If the shaman stood before the pale walls of the church, Hatilshay would see him even without the help of the moon. He watched the church, hoping that was the old one's plan.

A dog barked. They'd crept upwind to keep the village dogs from scenting them but what if one hunted in the field? Surely more than wind rustled the dry leaves behind him. Hatilshay wished his head could swivel completely around like an owl's or that his ears were far hearing as a rabbit's. As he wondered why Giver-of-Life had provided no such protection for The People, the door of the church opened. Hatilshay grunted in surprise.

How had the shaman gotten inside the church? His eyes must be deceiving him. It could not be the old one beside the Black Robe, yet who else of The People held his head as if searching the horizon?

The shaman moved from the square of yellow light and waited. The Black Robe hurried toward the mud-brick huts. Hatilshay's eyes watered as he strained to catch the movement of the shaman's arm. Surely now was the time to strike but he did not see the signal.

Hatilshay had convinced himself he'd missed it when the Black Robe returned with a Papago. Hatilshay's first thought was that the shaman had asked the Black Robe to deliver Chulito, but then he saw that this man was wide enough to make two of the young Papago.

The shaman and the Papago embraced as if they were cousins. The Black Robe made his magic sign in the air, returned to the church and closed the door behind him. The two men who should be enemies moved around the church, putting the building between themselves and the village. There they settled cross-legged and the glare of little Mexican cigars appeared.

Hatilshay leaned forward, hoping the wind would bring him their words. Babies cried, mothers sang and dogs yapped but not a murmur could Hatilshay hear from the men beside the church. The field swarmed with bugs and all of them bit. Hatilshay scratched the itches and rubbed spittle on the sore spots. The villagers went to sleep, a sliver of moon rose and still the men talked. Hatilshay wondered if the old one had forgotten their reason for coming. Perhaps, like his nephew, he'd seen bad omens and decided to leave Chulito for another time. Hatilshay had never heard of the shaman turning aside from a path he'd chosen but he could think of no other reason for the old one's strange actions. Then a thin arm raised and gestured.

Hatilshay rose and stumbled. Six or seven steps took the stiffness from his legs and he walked with more dignity. He crouched beside the two men, politely silent but searching the face of the stranger.

The Papago's face was too fat for wrinkles, but

there were deep creases by his mouth that came from much laughter. His eyes had some of the far-seeing look that the shaman's had.

"Speak the Mexican," said the old one. "Tell of your meeting with the Yankees."

"All?" Hatilshay did not want the Papago to learn of his foolish mistake with the yucca or the way he'd walked straight to the captain.

"Begin with the meeting of Chulito."

That was less shameful though it did nothing to build Hatilshay's fame as a clever warrior. He spoke truthfully of helping Turtlehead to the white-eye camp but gave none of his reasons for going. It made Turtlehead's wounds seem worse than they were but hid Hatilshay's distrust of his own eyes. He repeated all of Chulito's lies and most of Turtlehead's suspicions of witchcraft by both the white-eyes and himself. It was the truth. Also, the shaman had already heard it from Turtlehead. When he told of the long eye and watching Chulito drop from the wagon, followed by Bobcat Whiskers, the shaman raised his hand for silence.

"This my nephew did not tell me. It is my thought that Chulito did more than speak the insults."

The Papago's laugh lines deepened. "He was sent to learn the Yankee ways."

"You have Apache scalps in the village?"

The Papago's grin vanished. It was all the answer he gave, but it was enough.

"I ask the help of Chulito," said the shaman. "If he refuses help, all Apache scalps in the village will cry out. No ceremony will silence them. This I promise."

After a long silence, the Papago said, "There is this, old friend. Harm may come to Chulito. You have no scalps from my people. What can I raise to cry out against you?"

The shaman reached over and pulled four hairs from Hatilshay's head, one at a time. These he twisted and knotted, softly chanting a cradleboard song in the tongue of The People. He placed the knotted hairs on a square of painted buckskin, then repeated the ceremony with four hairs from his own head. Carefully he rolled the buckskin and tied it with a thong. As he offered the small bundle to the four directions, his voice raised in a song of the trickster coyote. One who did not understand the words could easily mistake it for a medicine song. Hatilshay kept his face muscles tense, afraid his inner laughter would break through.

The shaman gave the charm to the Papago. "Strike it four times with a rock, one time to each of the sacred directions. As the hairs are crushed, so will be the heads from which they came."

Hatilshay no longer had to hold back laughter. Fear crawled along his spine, though the shaman had sung no medicine songs.

The Papago looked as if he wished to return the rolled buckskin, but his fingers closed over it and he asked, "You have a place for the meeting?"

The shaman gave directions and they talked politely for a while. Hatilshay understood that in their youth the shaman and the Papago, like Chulito and himself, had been forced to put aside their weapons and travel together. In spite of their many repetitions of "old friend" and "my good friend," the shaman trusted the Papago no more than Hatilshay did Chulito. When they left the village, the old one took care to double back on their trail and cover all sign. It was a while before Hatilshay dared ask about the charm and then he had to circle around the question.

"I do not wish to have my head crushed," he said.

"Then take care to keep it from tight places," replied the shaman.

Hatilshay wondered if he was being teased. "The Papago has the charm."

"He has my promise. That is all the charm is. Old Pedito does not trust my word so I must give him a promise he can hold in his hand. It holds only the value I place on my word. If I planned to kill Chulito, the charm would make no difference."

"Then crushing the hairs will not kill us." Hatilshay did not receive the yes or no he wished for.

"It is easy for a man to believe that others are held by his own fears," said the shaman.

Hatilshay tried again. "Do the scalps truly cry out?"

"The Papagos hear them. Whole villages are kept awake and in fear until the few hairs of The People are fed and sung over. But there are people who take more than a few hairs from those they kill. They hear nothing, though they carry the scalps on their lances or ceremonial robes. I have thought that a scalp does not speak unless someone wishes to hear."

There was no time for more questions. They'd reached the rocks where Turtlehead was hidden. Immediately the shaman prepared the horse for travel.

"You have found the spirit carving," said Turtlehead.

"No," said his uncle. "We cannot find it without the Papago who speaks the white-eye tongue."

Though Turtlehead spoke to Hatilshay, his words were meant for the old one. "Why did you not bring him?"

The shaman answered. "We go to meet him."

Because of the darkness, Hatilshay was forced to walk near the horse and listen to Turtlehead's opinion of Chulito and his relatives, complaints on the stiffness of his legs and whether the night noises meant good or evil. To silence him, Hatilshay told how the shaman had cleverly used the Black Robe as messenger.

Turtlehead snorted. "It is well known that Black Robes welcome anyone."

"But I never heard of another using that knowledge."

"Who but my uncle has medicine strong enough to risk the Black Robe magic? I have heard their houses are filled with spirit carvings."

Mention of the carvings started his complaints again. Hatilshay trudged along wishing he had a charm made of Turtlehead's hair. Before they stopped, he'd changed that wish to a horse. The old one must have legs of iron.

They halted in a riverbed, a dangerous campsite so near the winter rains but the only place that would hide the horse and provide it with water. When Hatilshay climbed the steep bank at dawn, he discovered the ruins of a mud-brick building not far off. It was the meeting place, and from the banks they had a clear view in all directions. If the Papago betrayed them, they would not be trapped.

He slid down to the wide strip of sand between bank and water. He rubbed his right thigh and noticed Turtlehead watching.

"It twitches," he explained.

"That means a good journey," said Turtlehead.

Two days later they were still camped in the riverbed. Only the shaman was unworried.

"One man cannot speak for another," Hatilshay hinted. "Not even a Papago."

The shaman agreed, then added, "It may be that Chulito will have reasons of his own for guiding us."

"Reasons that mean no good for us," said Turtlehead.

His uncle continued as if he had not heard. "There is also this—my friend must travel to Chulito's village. He may not hurry so we will wait."

"We may wait too long. Already the stiffness creeps up my back."

"I will repeat the ceremony."

That left Hatilshay to watch alone. As he feared, a rider chose that time to appear, leading three horses. His warning interrupted the chant but the healing must have already begun, for Turtlehead climbed quickly to Hatilshay's side. The shaman remained seated, putting away his powders and feathers.

"Four horses, one rider." They were too distant for Hatilshay to risk naming the person.

"Is it Chulito?" asked the shaman.

Turtlehead scowled and muttered something about trouble. Hatilshay nodded to the old one before he realized any stranger would mean trouble to Turtlehead. He slid down the bank and followed the old one along the riverbed, uncertainty growing at every step. They climbed the bank near the tumbled building and found Chulito waiting. Hatilshay could have embraced him in relief.

"Where is the heathen with the blanket?" was the Papago's greeting.

"He waits." The shaman took two horses from Chulito and led them down river.

Chulito stared after him. "It is truly said that the Apache has no gratitude."

"It is well known that Apache legs are more strong than those of a horse," said Hatilshay.

"Not the heathen's." Chulito grinned as he tossed the reins of the riderless horse to Hatilshay. He kneed his mount after the shaman, but slowly so that Hatilshay could walk beside him. "It is for the heathen that I bring the horses. My father said, do not go without the sick one. If along the way he dies or becomes a tree, you will know and can turn back."

"Why should he become a tree?"

"Why should he not? Uam-ipudam became the green bark tree. The yellow blossoms are her dress."

Hatilshay could not imagine Turtlehead decked with spring flowers. A twisted mesquite, perhaps, or a chokeberry. Whatever the tree, its branches would wave frantically toward the Thunder People in every storm. Lightning-struck wood had great power. Hatilshay grinned as he thought of Turtlehead the tree.

"One of us is happy to see the Papago." Turtlehead's voice said also that it was just as he'd expected.

"I am happy because my right leg twitches like a horse with flies." The one lie inspired Hatilshay to others. "Also my ears ring and a lizard crossed my path."

As the words left his mouth, Hatilshay knew he was trapped. This was the wrong season for lizards. Why had he said such a stupid thing?

Turtlehead seemed not to have noticed. He asked, "Which way did it run?"

"Speak the Mexican," said Chulito. "I do not trust the heathen. No hairs were taken from his head."

Turtlehead answered in his own tongue. "And none will be. No fat grub of a white-eye slave can take my scalp."

"That is not what he meant," Hatilshay told him.

"Uncle, this savage thinks to kill us while we sleep!"

"He can't," said Hatilshay. "The Papagos fear the scalps."

"That does not stop this one from trying to take mine. Where hide the rest of your raiding party?"

"He cannot understand you."

Turtlehead only shouted louder, as if forcing the Papago to understand. And all the while Chulito shouted, "Speak the Mexican! Speak the Mexican!"

"We will speak what we please," Hatilshay yelled back, then called him a carrion-eating dog in Hopi. A wasted insult, for he remembered that only the old one could understand. Turtlehead was right. This Papago was trouble with a split tongue.

7

The
Naked
Savage

"Enough!" The shaman towered over them, his face dark as the clouds of the Thunder People. "We go!"

The old one had his bundles packed on his own horse before Hatilshay thought to help Turtlehead mount. The blanket-wearer looked bewildered at the old one's anger. The force of it silenced even Chulito. He stared when the shaman mounted a Papago horse and rode off leading his own, but said nothing until the meeting place was far behind.

"What does the old man lead, a horse or a bag of bones?" Chulito kept his voice pitched too low for the shaman's ears. "Truly the Apache knows nothing of horses. That one will not last the journey."

"That is true," said Hatilshay. "For when we have eaten the food it carries, we shall eat the horse. It will make poor eating but it is good for nothing else."

"Do not think to ride these horses until they drop,

then eat them. My father puts much value on horses. They must be returned."

"He can take this one now," Hatilshay told him.

The Papago grinned at him. "It gives me much sadness that my father had only one saddle."

A scrap of dirty blanket did little to soften the horse's spine and its coarse sweaty hair would soon rub his thighs raw. But these were not the reasons Hatilshay preferred to walk. Any unevenness of ground would hide a man but there were few places in the desert to hide four horses. Hatilshay glanced nervously at their back trail, then at two rocky hills to the southwest. He felt eyes in every direction, though he knew it was foolish.

"We go too fast," Chulito complained. "The horses must move slowly on such a long journey."

"How long?" Hatilshay asked.

Chulito jerked his shoulders. "Who knows? All the more reason to save the horses. Four horses my father sent and four horses he wants returned."

The shaman slowed their pace to a walk. Instead of approving, Chulito complained that the horses needed rest, though they stopped more often than Hatilshay thought necessary. To shorten their journey, the shaman cut across the river's many twists and turns. On the dry stretches, Chulito worried that the horses would die from lack of water. When they reached the river, he claimed they would founder from overdrinking.

"For what do you worry?" Hatilshay asked him. "It will not stop the horse from stepping in a hole and breaking a leg. Better to ride it at top speed. The end is the same."

Chulito glared at him. "These horses will not break legs nor will they be used badly."

"Horses are good only for speed."

"For the heathen, any pace is speed."

That was true. If Turtlehead was put on foot, they would not move at all. Hatilshay kept his opinions on horse care to himself.

They were traveling a dry stretch at sunset and did not camp until they again reached the river. Once more Chulito warned against letting the horses drink their fill. When Hatilshay dragged his from the water, the Papago had unsaddled his horse and staked it. As it cropped the scant grass, Chulito brushed its flanks.

"Will you also braid feathers in the mane?" asked Hatilshay.

"I had not thought of it, though the Yankees put ribbons in the mane and tail."

Hatilshay moved closer and saw that he was serious. "Was all this care of horses learned from the Yankees?"

Chulito gave him a strange look and nodded.

"Is the horse a Yankee clan symbol?" Hatilshay could think of no other reason for such foolishness, though none of The People worried so about their animal symbols.

"The Yankees are civilized. It is their way to care for things."

The scorn in his voice angered Hatilshay. "If you have such love of Yankee ways, you should have stayed with them."

"I wish that I had!"

Before Hatilshay could recover from his surprise, Chulito ducked under the horse's belly and put the animal between them. The shaman had said that Chulito might have his own reasons for guiding them to the white-eye wagon. It would seem that he was right.

Hatilshay looked for a place to tie his horse. He did not understand why he couldn't tie two legs together as he had with the old one's horse. Staking horses must be another Yankee way. He was so deep in his thoughts that he jumped at Turtlehead's voice.

"Tell me what you saw," said Turtlehead. "The lizard that crossed your path, which way did it run?"

The horse strained to reach a saltbush. Hatilshay let it pull him around, giving himself time to remember what Turtlehead was talking about. He waved his free hand.

"North," said Turtlehead. "The way you walked then, that would be north. It is a sign that you must travel north."

"If the lizard ran, it was frightened."

"A frightened lizard would run from you, not across your path."

"A lizard didn't run anywhere. They sleep under rocks and underground at this season." Hatilshay had now admitted he'd lied but he might as well not have spoken.

"True," Turtlehead admitted. "But they come out to sun themselves on warm days."

"The days have not been that warm."

"Which proves the importance of the message. The

lizard was wakened to guide you. It is clear you must go north but I do not understand the ringing in your ears."

Hatilshay groaned. What had put such foolish words on his tongue? And why had he spoken them? Turtlehead must have thought of nothing else all day. Hatilshay was truly glad when Chulito pushed him aside.

"The horse must be staked properly. I will do it." The Papago looked suspiciously at Turtlehead. "What does he plot now?"

"He wants only to learn what causes the ears to ring," Hatilshay told him.

"The bells of the church when you stand too near."

Hatilshay translated to be sure Turtlehead understood. It would give him something to occupy his thoughts that night.

The Papago had brought dried meat, as tough to chew as the dried mescal the shaman had packed. Chulito also had a bag of dried corn but it needed boiling and he had forgotten a pot.

"I will save it for the horses," said the Papago. "They may need it before the journey is finished."

Hatilshay drew away to speak with the shaman in their own tongue. "The Papago plans for a long journey."

"The Papago doesn't know where we go." The old one smiled and gave Hatilshay no chance to ask his question. "If he is right, the soldiers go to the fort by the big river."

"Where the dreamers live?"

The shaman nodded. "I traveled this way with Pedito long ago. There was no fort then."

"If you know the way, there is no need for the Papago."

"Who will speak with the white-eyes when we find them? Who will take us inside the fort?" He looked as he had when correcting Hatilshay's Mexican, long ago when he'd taught him the tongue. "I can lead us to the fort but the Papago must find the carving."

They mounted at first light, as travelers should. Toward the end of the day they passed cone-shaped hills whose sides were covered with black stones. They reminded Hatilshay of anthills but the ants would have to be large as horses. Had some giant covered the hills with stones? How else had they come there, as if rolled from the top just as ants rolled dirt from their holes. When they stopped to rest the horses, Hatilshay discovered the rocks were pitted and weighed more for their size than they should.

"Stones of the Thunder People," the shaman told him. But he could not say how they'd come to cover the strangely shaped hills.

The following day brought wind. Dust cones whirled over the land on spindly bases, collapsing when they reached the river and reforming on the other side. As each dust spirit appeared, Chulito crossed himself and muttered. The wind strengthened, filling the air with dust and sand. The horizon disappeared in a dirty haze. Even worse, the flat land was strewn thick with the heavy pitted rocks. The horses picked their way around them. Hatilshay hunched over, eyes narrowed against the dust, and followed the flank of Chulito's horse.

The wind faded with the light, leaving them wind-burned and covered with dust. All except Turtlehead, who had huddled under his blanket. Hatilshay wasted no time watering and staking his horse. He slipped a thong over its front legs, then stripped off his shirt and loincloth and waded into the river. The water was cold but he'd often broken ice to swim in the mountains.

Cold water and snow were said to keep hair from growing. Perhaps that was the reason the white-eyes were covered with hair. From their smell, they must not swim from one season to the next.

Chulito and the shaman joined him. As they dressed, Chulito said, "I see no stars in the north. There will be rain."

It reached them before morning. They woke wet and shivering, ready to travel since they could not sleep. For a second day they rode in silence. When their passing startled quail from hiding, Hatilshay dismounted and helped the Papago run down four. The exercise warmed him for a time and when his body again chilled, he had the thought of roast meat to cheer him.

The rain stopped late in the day but low heavy clouds hid the sunset and the wind had the bite of snow. Turtlehead shed his sodden blanket. Hatilshay and the shaman stripped off their buckskin shirts, though Hatilshay did not look forward to putting his on after it dried. Only Chulito, who wore heavy cloth trousers as well as a shirt, remained fully clothed. As they watered the horses, Hatilshay heard the Papago's teeth chattering.

"Wind on bare skin is less cold than wind through wet cloth," he told Chulito.

"Naked savages," was his answer.

From behind them, the shaman's voice said quietly, "Even the civilized catch the coughing sickness if they sleep in wet clothes."

Chulito stopped rubbing down his horse long enough to undress. Beneath the shirt and trousers he was truly naked, without even a loincloth. Hatilshay glanced at the shaman and quickly hid his smile. Turtlehead laughed and the naked Chulito glared at him. It was a look that reminded Hatilshay never to trust a Papago. When he scattered the fire to warm and dry the ground for sleeping, Hatilshay wished a live coal would find its way under Chulito. If one did, the Papago made no complaint.

They began the next day cold, tired and wet. No rain had fallen, but the damp air had not dried their clothes. Chulito carefully put one leg into his wet trousers and grimaced.

"You will get the coughing sickness," Hatilshay warned him.

"A civilized man does not go naked."

Hatilshay laughed. "How is it that you have the civilizing and I have the loincloth?"

The Papago looked mad enough to bite. Hatilshay moved quickly to help Turtlehead mount.

"We are near the white-eyes," Turtlehead said. "I know, for the stiffness is growing."

"It is the dampness," Hatilshay told him. "We are all stiff this morning."

"It is not the same." He looked as angry as the Papago.

"There is clear sky to the northwest. We may have sun today."

Turtlehead kicked his horse forward without answering; the news did not seem to cheer anyone except Hatilshay.

They left the river for the last time. It flowed deeper and stronger from the rains, with clouds over the mountains promising heavier run-off. Enough pools remained in the desert to supply them with water but it was unnatural for the Papago not to complain. Nor did Turtlehead speak of omens or remind Hatilshay that he should be traveling north. The blanket-wearer did not speak at all except to refuse to dismount at rest stops. When they camped for the night, Chulito and Hatilshay had to lift him from his horse.

"Are we near the white-eyes?" he asked his uncle.

In Mexican, the shaman said, "We reach the Yankee village tomorrow."

Turtlehead gave Hatilshay a triumphant look. "I have felt it all day."

Hatilshay gazed past him at the Papago's face. He'd seen that look before, when Chulito had pointed an arrow at his heart. He wished to warn the shaman but had no chance, for after they'd eaten and rested the horses and the shaman had chanted over Turtlehead, they traveled most of the night. What remained of it the shaman spent in chanting again. A short journey before full light brought them within sight of a wide, muddy river. The one they'd followed flowed into this one somewhere to the north. Hatilshay could just make out the square shadows that meant buildings.

"You will go with the Papago to the village," the shaman had told him. "When you learn where the spirit carving has been taken, return here."

He had not waited for Hatilshay's protests but had gone to sing over his nephew. While Chulito rubbed down the horses, Hatilshay took his bow from its case, inspected it carefully before stringing and then selected his best arrows. When the shaman's high voice stopped, Hatilshay moved over to the red and yellow bundle that was Turtlehead.

"I do not trust the Papago," he whispered. "How am I to know what he tells the white-eyes?"

"Must you have a promise you can touch?" The old one's voice was weak from chanting but it carried enough scorn to heat Hatilshay's face. "Would you trust the Papago if you made a charm from the hair of his head?"

The bundle stirred as Turtlehead raised himself on one elbow. "You know of such a charm?" he asked Hatilshay.

"Yes."

"It has great power?"

"Its power is uncertain," answered the shaman, though his eyes remained on Hatilshay.

"The Papago would fear it," Hatilshay argued.

"Fear alone does not hold a man."

"Your Papago friend feared the scalps in his village."

"That is true. But if he had planned treachery, fear would not have stopped him. He would have told himself that the scalps might not cry out. Or if they did, gifts and songs would quiet them. A man tells himself many strange things and finds them believable."

"Still, he sent Chulito."

"He went to speak with him," corrected the shaman. "And he spoke for us because he came to suspect that Chulito had helped Bobcat Whiskers. At the last, it comes always to a man's honor." The old one's eyes crinkled at the corners. "But fear sometimes helps a man to remember his honor."

"I would like to remind the Papago of his."

"He has none," said Turtlehead. "Make the charm."

Then he moaned, pulled the medicine blanket over his head and lay back.

Hatilshay knew a charm was useless, for the Papago had been taught by Black Robes and white-eyes. He could argue against charms in three tongues and if the Papago had no fear, the charm had no power. Hatilshay grunted as he turned that thought end for end.

Did Bobcat Whiskers' carving have power only because Turtlehead feared it? And the blanket, did its medicine come only from Turtlehead's belief? Then what of White Painted Lady, the Thunder People and Giver-of-Life himself? If one stopped believing, did they vanish like smoke? Just tell one's heart, I do not believe, and poof! the gods are gone. Could it be true?

He glanced at the shaman and met the wise road-runner look. If the old one truly knew the terrible place his thoughts had carried him, he might . . . . Hatilshay almost laughed aloud. Let the shaman chant his spells. They were no more real than half the things his eyes told him. All the same, he was glad the Papago came to hunker beside them.

"The horses cannot travel for a time," said Chulito. "The village must wait."

"You can leave the horses here," said the shaman. "I will care for them."

Chulito stiffened and eyed the old one suspiciously. "You want to keep the horses."

"I gave my promise to care for you. Evil people may live in that village. I would not have them steal the horses. Leave them with me until you return." The shaman leaned forward, his eyes glinting with laughter. "You will return here?"

The anger in Chulito's face showed he understood. If he wished to keep the horses, he must speak the truth and return with Hatilshay. The Papago eyed Hatilshay's bow, then glared at the shaman.

"I will return." He rose and hitched up his trousers. "Let us go."

He strode up the slight rise that sheltered them from view of the village. Straight across the open land he marched and Hatilshay had no choice but to follow, feeling naked and helpless as a slow bug on a flat rock.

The village had no high protecting walls. The wide

bumpy path they followed led between buildings. Hatilshay counted them on the fingers of one hand. A few tents had been raised but no soldiers could be seen. Yet surely it was a war camp for there were no cook fires, women or children. There were men, though, hairy and red-faced as soldiers but without the blue suits.

Chulito spoke to one and was answered with a shove that sent him staggering across the road. Hatilshay drew back against a mud-brick building and hoped no one would notice him. The Papago fool not only stayed in the open, he approached another white-eye. The man jerked a thumb over his shoulder toward the river. Chulito stared in that direction, then turned and ran after the man, jogging beside him as they spoke. The man pushed him aside and ducked into one of the tents. The Papago turned, stared down the dusty road at the river, then he looked at Hatilshay and laughed.

Hatilshay groped for the bag of sacred pollen before he remembered that there were no gods. He was alone. Except for a happy Papago.

8

Poor Lo

"This money makes no sense," Hatilshay told the Papago. "If the man with the boat is hungry, why does he not ask for food?"

"He may get too much and it will go bad."

"He can give it to others."

"Then what will he do tomorrow if no one wishes to cross the river?"

"It may be that tomorrow some person will give food to the man in the boat."

"It may not be, also," said Chulito. "That is the good thing with money. Money does not go bad. There is no need to give anything to others."

Hatilshay was shocked. Not even from a Papago did he expect such selfishness. "Is this money a Yankee way?"

"All the civilized use it."

It was a Yankee way. From what Hatilshay knew of the Papago, it was not a way Chulito's people would approve. Truly, Chulito must have been eager to lead this journey. His selfish white-eye ways must have set him apart much as a charge of witchcraft would have put Hatilshay aside from his own people. He felt a quick sympathy for the Papago which he tried to smother.

Hatilshay rose and led Chulito around the white-eye buildings toward the river. The Papago had learned that the soldiers lived in a walled fort on the other side, but to cross the river, one must give money to a man with a boat. Hatilshay could not see the fort but he did not doubt that it was there. Chulito had been too happy with the news. But he did not understand why they must use the boat to cross. Not until he stood on the bank.

The river was wide as some mountain valleys and the current flowed as if in full flood. As Hatilshay watched, a dead tree passed, the tangle of roots dipping and turning. They could not swim here but perhaps there was a place farther up.

There wasn't. By the time Hatilshay admitted it, they were caked to the knees with mud and mosquito bites swelled their faces. They left the swampy river shores and climbed a ridge, dry and sunny enough to rid them of flying swamp bugs. Without a word, they threw themselves down to rest. They'd lain there long enough for the mud to dry on Hatilshay's moccasins when Chulito said, "Now we go home?"

"Do your people still wait for tales of the Yankee wonders?" Hatilshay immediately regretted his teasing. Not even a Papago should look that bitter when reminded of home.

"They sent me to learn the Yankee ways. Then they say to forget them. Our ways are better, they say. What do we care for the Yankees?"

Though Hatilshay thought the same, he did not say so. Instead he asked, "Why, then, were you sent?"

"My uncle sent me. He was head man of our village but he died while I was away."

Hatilshay caught his breath at the casual mention of death, as if the uncle had been an animal and not a man. Then Chulito crossed himself in the way of the Black Robes and Hatilshay remembered that Papagos had learned Mexican ways long before white-eyes had come.

"My uncle thought it wise to learn the Yankee ways," Chulito continued.

"For what?"

"He had been told that this land belongs to the Yankees."

Hatilshay laughed.

"It is true!" said the Papago.

"No man can own the land. He can use it while he walks and farms and hunts. The Yankees do not even do that." In all the raiding and hunting territory of his village, Hatilshay knew of only two white-eye ranches. From time to time white-eyes roamed the mountains, digging in the ground or trapping beaver. But, like the soldiers, they did not stay.

"They do not use the land," he repeated. "And there are so few."

"Few here but in their villages they are countless. They will come like the white moths in summer." The Papago's voice turned proud. "And when they come, I will be friend to the Yankee, for I know their ways. I will ride the iron monsters and help them to smoke out the heathen Apache."

Whatever sympathy Hatilshay had felt vanished. No doubt Chulito had spoken this way to his own people. He deserved to be shunned. All the same, talk of white-eye swarms made Hatilshay uneasy. He stopped picking at the dried mud on his moccasins and squinted at the land about them. A square shape at the north edge of the ridge reminded him of the church in the Papago village.

"Look, is that not a bell tower?" he asked.

Chulito answered with insults about the heathen savages living along the river, to which Hatilshay did not listen. The old one had received help from the Black Robes. Surely they must have a boat, alone here by the river. He scrambled to his feet and trotted toward the tower.

"Where do you go?" shouted the Papago.

"To find help."

Chulito laughed. A warning stirred between Hatilshay's ribs, the feeling that all was not right and his eyes had betrayed him again. They had. The tower had no roof and one wall of the building had fallen. Hatilshay slowed to a walk, wondering what reason he could give that would not make him appear foolish. Through the empty windows he could see green leaves. The Black Robes had been gone a long time. There could be nothing inside for him to find and say he had come for, no answer to Chulito's insults.

He glanced over his shoulder. The Papago had followed, but slowly. Because he could think of no other way to escape Chulito's sharp tongue, Hatilshay circled the building. Where fallen brick had left a gap in the thick wall, Hatilshay caught the scent of roasting meat. Not horse nor any game he'd ever smelled, but strong and most certainly meant to be eaten.

Selecting footholds with care, he climbed the heap of rubble and peered around the edge of the opening. Dark shapes startled him until he realized they were only places where the painted plaster had fallen from an inner wall. The fire and its builder might be safely beyond that wall. Then again, the cook might be waiting just behind the wall where Hatilshay crouched. He did not care to risk his head by looking. Nor did he like the thought of passing in front of the gap. Better to retreat to firm ground, circle the opening and approach for a look from the other side.

As he drew back, the brick beneath his shoulder moved. He grabbed for it, his foot slipped and broken bricks skittered down the heap. The dust made Hatilshay sneeze and he gave up any hope of being mistaken for a curious animal. Should he leap through the wall like a raiding party or should he turn and run? A yell from inside decided him to run, then he heard the words and remembered Chulito.

"Stupid Papago," he muttered and scrambled through the opening.

A rattler gave warning and Hatilshay leaped for the arch in the painted wall. He skidded through, tried to pull himself upright and instead added force to his stumbling lunge. What he hit was warm, hairy and well muscled. It reared and whinnied. Hatilshay grabbed a handful of mane and kept on his feet.

"My horse," yelled Chulito.

A deeper voice, just as angry, ordered, "Let go the horse!"

Hatilshay would have willingly obeyed if the horse had let him but it lunged forward and back, trying to escape from between Hatilshay and the wall. Other bodies collided with the frightened animal, jostling and pushing until Hatilshay feared he would fall beneath the hoofs. He ducked under a naked brown arm, tripped over a trousered leg and was at last free to stand or run. Before choosing, he inspected the small room.

Opposite the arch he'd entered, the Papago and a stranger hauled on the horse, which did appear to be Chulito's, then shouted at each other in several tongues. The roof had not fallen and the light was dim but Hatilshay did not need to see to know that the horse had been kept here a long time. There was also another smell, one Hatilshay did not know.

A square opening led to another room, also roofed.

And from the appearance of the dirt floor, also long occupied. Hatilshay moved cautiously around the walls to the door leading to the bell tower, then to an arch leading to the weed-grown part of the ruin. Chulito must have come that way, surprising the stranger at his cook fire. The carcass of some animal still roasted just inside the archway. It seemed a lot of meat for one stranger. Hatilshay returned to the first room.

The horse had calmed but Chulito and the stranger still clung to it. The insults were now all in Mexican.

"Dirty heathen," said Chulito.

Hatilshay half agreed with him. The stranger wore only a ragged loincloth and sandals. His hair hung loose, uncombed and matted with dirt. Hatilshay drew the knife from his moccasin and pressed the point against the stranger's bare back.

He yelped.

"How many are with you?" Hatilshay asked in Mexican.

"Alone." The head turned. He tried to smile. "Now you come. Friends, no?"

"No," said Chulito.

"Move." Hatilshay waved both of them toward the other room.

Though his shoulders were broad and heavily muscled, the stranger was young as Hatilshay and Chulito. He crouched by the meat, still grinning. "Eat. Very good."

Chulito cut a chunk, sniffed and tasted it. "Where do you get sheep?"

"Sheep this big? Have fur not good and smell bad?"
The Papago nodded.

"That sheep," said the stranger.

Hatilshay cut a chunk of meat and sat with his back
to one side of the arch, trying to watch all approaches
while he ate.

"Where did you steal the sheep?" Chulito asked.

"Not steal." There was more laughter in the voice
than insult. "Men bring many tens of sheep over river.
Sheep all together. Make much noise, big smell. Sheep
very stupid. One bark of coyote, all run."

"And you find," said Chulito.

"Yes, bring to men. They give sheep for work."

Chulito helped himself to more meat. He'd almost
finished it before he asked, "How long past was this?"

"One moon. Maybe more."

"And this sheep was not killed until now?"

"Sheep very stupid." The stranger waved at the horse
room. "Some get in there. Not get out."

Hatilshay laughed.

"Thief," shouted Chulito.

"Liar," said the stranger.

Deliberately waving his knife, Hatilshay moved between them and cut more meat. He was scarcely settled
at his sentry post before the Papago said, "The horse,
it is very stupid. It came in here and could not get out."

"Yes! You know." The stranger rocked backward in
laughter.

Hatilshay heard a rustle and caught movement from
the corner of his eye. He turned only to see the bottom

of a trouser leg disappear into the other room. The stranger must not have seen that much, for he sat up and looked around as if bewildered. Hatilshay had not thought Chulito could move so fast but it seemed only a few breaths before the horse pounded through the open part of the ruin, past the arch and out the weed-grown door. Would the Papago return to the old one or keep riding? Hatilshay did not care to place a wager either way.

"Very bad," said the stranger. "Now boat come, no horse."

"Boat?" Hatilshay lost all interest in what Chulito might do. "The boat to cross the river, it comes here?"

"That boat nothing." He waved it aside with a scornful gesture. "Big boat come every moon. Maybe later, maybe not so late. Big boat, big wheel. Chung-ka-chung-ka-chung!"

The stranger circled his hand to the sound. "Ka-chung-ka-chung! Wheel turn, make big splash. Big smoke make whoooo-whooooo!"

He threw back his head like a coyote and the shrill whistle echoed from the belfry and the bare walls. Hatilshay's ears didn't ring but the sound reminded him of his lie to Turtlehead. Certainly he'd come north along the river and found a belfry. He shook his head to clear his thoughts, not his hearing. All the same, the blanket-wearer's reading of Hatilshay's lie had come very near the truth. To avoid thinking about it, Hatilshay asked, "For what do you need the horse?"

"Tell the Yankees the boat comes."

After much questioning, Hatilshay learned the wheel boat came north up the big river, past the Yankee town and fort, past the abandoned church and then farther north, eastward on another river. The same river, Hatilshay guessed, that they had followed from the meeting with the Papago. If they had stayed on its bank, they would have found another Yankee town. A new one and very rich, according to the stranger.

"River bad for boats. Sometimes very bad, sometimes not so bad. Faster go by horse. Tell Yankee wheel boat come."

"For what?" asked Hatilshay. "When it comes, they know."

"Yankees very stupid, like sheep. Boat comes, all run. Like ants, they stand. Stand all day for little paper from boat."

"The paper has writing?" Hatilshay tried to explain what he meant.

"Who is to know?" said the stranger. "Who is to care? Rich Yankee not like to stand all day. Cousin make trade. Cousin sit in line, rich Yankee give food. Cousin sit one, two, three day. Good trade."

Hatilshay eyed the belfry stairs. "And where is the cousin?"

"Ah." It was half groan, half sigh. For the first time, the stranger looked truly sad. He nodded south, toward the town and fort. "Yankees there say cousin steal horse. Hang cousin."

With one hand, he pulled upward on an invisible rope. His head lolled to one side, eyes staring and tongue hanging out. Then he straightened and sighed.

"Spirit not get out mouth. Cousin not in spirit world. Not anywhere. Very sad." His eyes brightened and he grinned. "Then wagons come. Many wagons, many soldiers. Too many horses. One night big bang!"

The stranger clapped his hands together and laughed. "Horses all run."

The stranger and his friends had taken the horses back to the soldiers and been given food and presents for their help. When the wagons had traveled on, the stranger had found a horse tied to a tree. Hatilshay smelled a lie.

"Who would leave a horse tied to a tree?" he asked.

"Maybe same person what make big bang."

Hatilshay grinned. "When was this?"

"Three, four days past."

"The wagons, where did they go?" They must be the same ones. The time was right and the stranger had said there were soldiers. "Can you take us to the wagons?"

"Must wait for wheel boat."

"You have no horse," Hatilshay reminded him. "You cannot race the boat to the town without a horse."

The stranger stared into the fire and said nothing.

"Lead us to the wagons. When we find the wagons, it may be you will find another horse."

The stranger looked up. "You make big bang, find horse?"

Hatilshay remembered the well-guarded white-eye camp and said cautiously, "Perhaps."

"Two horses," bargained the stranger.

"Two horses and you must help with the stealing."

"Three horses, much help."

Hatilshay suspected he was being stampeded like the sheep and horses. A few ill-chosen words and he'd be pledged to steal a whole herd for this wily trader. As he considered a counter offer, Hatilshay heard the soft thud of horse hoofs. He stiffened and moved back from the arch, his knife ready. For a short time he heard nothing, then again the hoofbeats, this time with footsteps. Not the step of a sensible man, cautious even when approaching his own camp, but the heavy tread of one who never thought of danger. A white-eye step.

9

White-Eye
Town

Chulito led the horse through weeds and bushes growing in the open part of the ruins. He stopped outside the arch and peered in at the stranger.

"I ask pardon," he said. "This is not my horse."

Hatilshay was furious. When at last the Papago had been of some help, he came back to spoil it. How could Hatilshay bargain with the stranger after his horse was returned?

"It looks like your horse," said Hatilshay. "Even the scars on the flank are the same. Surely two horses would not be wounded in the same way."

Chulito looked as if he'd caught a bad smell. "All soldiers' horses look much the same. They are of the finest. And the scars are the mark of the Yankees."

Hatilshay remembered that Papago women made

scars on their chins and thought themselves beautiful. Perhaps the white-eyes also took pride in such marks, though it seemed foolish to put them on horses. The animals were too easily lost or stolen.

"It is not my horse," Chulito said again.

He might be speaking the truth, but for Hatilshay to admit it would lose their guide to the wagons. True, the old one or even Hatilshay himself could find the new white-eye town, but only after a long search. The stranger could lead them quickly by the shortest path.

"I say this is your horse," Hatilshay told Chulito. "When we find the old one and the rest of the horses, we will know."

"The old one has many horses?" asked the stranger.

"The horses are my father's," Chulito told him.

The stranger grinned at Hatilshay. "You spoke truth. No good stay here. Poor Lo go find wagons, get horse."

Hatilshay stared at him. "Is it your way to give names as freely as meat?" If so, Poor Lo would be asking for Hatilshay's in return.

Chulito laughed. "Poor Lo is not his name."

"It is what he calls himself." said Hatilshay.

"It is what the Yankees call the Indians."

"Are the Indians a band of the Yuma?" Hatilshay had guessed that the stranger was one of the people for whom the old one had named him, the ones called Yuma in the Mexican.

"Stupid one," said Chulito. "Yuma is Indian. Apache is Indian."

The Yuma grinned at Hatilshay. "Indian is Poor Lo."

Though he could not think how it could be, Hatilshay suspected them of making him appear a fool. He was certain of it when Chulito said, "Lo, the poor Indian," and the Yuma replied in the white-eye tongue.

Hatilshay interrupted their jabbering with, "Speak the Mexican!"

"His people trade always with the Yankees," Chulito explained. "He is easier with that tongue than with the Mexican."

Hatilshay wondered how strongly the old one felt about his promise to return Chulito safely. If Poor Lo spoke the white-eye tongue, what need had they for the Papago? The same thought must have found Chulito for he added quickly, "He speaks it poor as the blanket-wearer speaks the Mexican. And it is said that the river ran with sand when last a Yuma spoke the truth."

Hatilshay had heard the same said of the Papago. Truly, there seemed little difference between them except that the old one had ways to keep the Papago faithful.

"Let us find the old one," said Hatilshay.

Poor Lo agreed eagerly. "Find the old one with horses."

Chulito glared at him, a reminder that peace between Yuma and Papago had always been a sometime thing. Feeling more cheerful, Hatilshay led the way through the ruins. Poor Lo followed, then Chulito, leading the horse. Remembering the rattle he'd heard before, Hatilshay took care in choosing a path through the rubble.

This was the season for snakes to sleep but the day was warm as spring, warm enough to coax snakes and lizards into the sun. In this low warm land, perhaps they did not sleep at all. Though his attention was on his feet, Hatilshay heard Chulito complain about leaving the roasted sheep.

"No matter," said Poor Lo. "Find more soon."

"We have food," Hatilshay said. "We have that horse. You say it is not yours."

And perhaps it wasn't, for Chulito said only, "It is wasteful to leave good meat."

"Wasteful, wasteful," chanted Poor Lo. "Wasteful Indian. Not good Indian."

"Is Papago Indian?" asked Hatilshay.

"The Papago are good Christians," said Chulito.

Soon after, he rode past Hatilshay. The horse put him head and shoulders over the squat trees.

"You make a good target," said Hatilshay.

"Yankees see you," said Poor Lo. "Say you steal horse. Hang like cousin."

Hatilshay kept his eyes forward. He'd already seen Poor Lo act the hanging, his head lolled to one side and his tongue hanging out. Chulito looked, though, and the sight gave him caution, for he dismounted and led the horse.

As they circled the white-eye town, with the fort of soldiers on the opposite shore, Hatilshay strained eyes and ears. Poor Lo seemed alert and wary, also, but the Papago clumped along uncaring. They were scarcely out of sight of the roofs when Chulito remounted and led the way to where the old one waited. He pointed a finger at the browsing horses and said, "You see. I spoke the truth."

"Yes," Hatilshay admitted, though something about the horses bothered him.

The Yuma tugged at Chulito's sandaled foot. "Poor Lo take horse. Go now."

"Wait," said Hatilshay.

"No wait. Go watch for steamboat."

"But it will soon be dark. Do you travel when the spirits walk?"

"Spirits walk all time," said the Yuma.

"Heathen superstition," sneered Chulito.

"Go brush the horses," Hatilshay told him. Then he knew what had bothered him about the horses. "There are only four."

"But yes," said the Papago. He slid from the horse but Hatilshay crowded him against the animal's side. At best it could be only a short delay, for the Yuma was preparing to mount from the other side. Hatilshay searched frantically for another argument. Fear of spirits would not keep Poor Lo with them, not if what the old one said of the Yuma was true. If Poor Lo truly walked in the land of spirits and held council with the gods, Hatilshay's fears were as smoke.

Poor Lo sniffed noisily. Hatilshay turned his face to the light breeze and knew as surely as if he'd watched the old one cut its neck which of the horses was missing.

"You speak true," said Poor Lo. "Sun go. Poor Lo stay. We eat and talk, no?"

The Yuma followed his nose quickly to where the meat roasted.

A small fire had been made behind a rise, out of sight of the white-eye town.

"Eat quickly," said the old one. "We want no fire when the sun is gone."

Poor Lo snatched a piece of seared meat from the cooking stones set in the fire. Turtlehead came from under his blanket to stare.

"What is this one?" he asked in the tongue of The People. "Another enemy so that we dare not sleep?"

In the same tongue, Hatilshay told him, "He knows where the wagons have gone. We must keep him with us."

"That does not seem a problem," said the old one as he watched Poor Lo drop fresh chunks of horsemeat on the hot stones.

"It may be difficult." Hatilshay told what had been said at the ruined church.

The old one's laugh lines deepened and his mouth twitched, but he said nothing. Turtlehead muttered about lizards and omens and ringing in the ears. Chulito tended the horses, speaking either to himself or to them. Hatilshay speared a piece of meat on his knife. Turtlehead reached for it with both hands. Hatilshay saw that the left one had turned green, blue and dirty yellow.

"Does it give much pain?" asked Hatilshay.

With his right hand, Turtlehead rubbed the mottled coloring. "When pain is seen, it is not felt."

"Is that true?" Hatilshay asked the old one, for the hand was swollen and looked very painful.

"Pain will come later," said the shaman.

"The stiffness comes now," said his nephew, though he stuffed his mouth quickly enough and twice reached pieces of meat before Poor Lo, who stopped eating only to refill the cooking stones. Chulito finished tending the horses and joined them.

"Do not think to eat my father's horses," he warned. Twice as he ate he said, "Horsemeat is not a food for the civilized."

"Is fish?" Hatilshay spat to get even the word from his mouth, for The People ate no creature that lived in water.

"Fish good!" said Poor Lo. "Sun come, we get much fish, no?"

"No!" shouted Hatilshay.

With a moan, Turtlehead pulled the blanket around his head.

"Stupid heathen," said Chulito. "The priests eat fish. Why should not the Yankees?"

"Stupid Yankees," Hatilshay told him. "Not to eat horsemeat."

They had so many, a few horses would not be missed, and it was easier than hunting ground squirrels with a net on a stick.

Poor Lo stared at Chulito. "You like Yankees? Yankees not like you."

"What do you know of the Yankees?" Chulito's voice was full of scorn but Poor Lo seemed not to notice. With short pauses to find words and longer ones to chew and swallow, the Yuma told how his people had once earned many shirts and blankets taking Yankees across the river. Then one night Yankees attacked and broke up the raft. Now only white-eyes took horses and people across the river.

"How did your people get the raft?" asked Chulito. "The same way you got the horse and sheep?"

Poor Lo grinned. "One time kill Yankees, take back raft. Then soldiers come. No more raft for Poor Lo." He slapped his upper arm. "Yankees like mosquitos. Kill two, three, much more come." He waved toward the sunset.

"Yankees live to the east." Hatilshay also waved so the Yuma would not mistake his meaning.

They argued about it until Chulito said, "Yankees have towns on both oceans. The richest live there." He pointed westward. "They dig gold and have all the finest things sent from the grand villages in the east. Wagons and ships full of wonders and riches."

"Steamboat come," agreed Poor Lo.

"Bigger than steamboat," said Chulito. "I cannot tell how big."

"Steamboat," repeated Poor Lo. "Steamboat, wagons go up river."

"Wagons go across river to San Francisco."

"Up," argued Poor Lo. "All same place."

From beneath the medicine blanket Turtlehead said in his own tongue, "We must follow this new person. It is as the omen showed us. You went north to the place of bells and found help."

Hatilshay snorted. "When last you spoke of the omen, you did not know the meaning."

"I can read the meaning now."

"Any fool can find a trail that is already marked."

Chulito ordered, "Speak the Mexican. I wish to know what my friends plot."

The Yuma bent forward to peer at Turtlehead. "You like Yankees?"

Hatilshay answered. "He holds no love for the Yankees and there is reason." Then he told of the spirit carving and Turtlehead's growing stiffness. Perhaps the Yuma would stay with them out of hatred for the Yankees.

"We must find the wagons quickly," Hatilshay said. "Will you guide us to them?"

"Three horses, no help?" bargained Poor Lo.

The old one spoke softly, suggesting the Yuma speak with someone with a name that was gargled, adding, "Long ago we hunted together."

"I ask," said Poor Lo and stretched out beside the fire, which Hatilshay killed.

They should have moved some distance before sleeping, in case white-eyes had seen their fire, but Poor Lo was already asleep and Turtlehead appeared to be. Even when awake, it was difficult to move the blanket-wearer. What Poor Lo had said about white-eyes kept Hatilshay awake, for it was the opposite of what Chulito claimed. Hatilshay did not believe either lied, for even The People did not agree on the nature of white-eyes. Why did they behave like two different peoples? Perhaps the ones in the east were different from the ones in the west. He hoped this was true, for he would not like The People to be caught between two peoples such as the Yuma claimed white-eyes to be.

Hatilshay was certain Poor Lo did not move during the night, yet in the morning he woke, stretched and announced that the one with the gargled name said go. It was as clear as one of Turtlehead's omens.

"Go where?" asked Hatilshay.

"To wagons. Good trade there."

"When were you told this?" Hatilshay crawled about, looking for trail sign. "No one came here. You did not move."

"Go spirit mountain," said Poor Lo.

"There is no such place," said Chulito. "There is only heaven and hell."

They began an argument that lasted until they were all mounted and following the shaman and Turtlehead. Hatilshay lagged behind, listening to the Yuma and Papago argue about the creation of the world.

"I know," Poor Lo insisted. "I there. I see."

Chulito snorted.

"I there! I see Blind Old Man make mud people. Have duck feet, no hands. How Poor Lo know if not there?"

"Someone told you."

"I there! All my people there, see from time of all water."

"They dream it," said Hatilshay. He knew that much from the old one's stories. "Each boy dreams everything from the beginning of the world."

"Each boy dreams the same dream?" said Chulito. "This I do not believe."

"Some dream wrong," Poor Lo admitted. "Old man tell them, no, this happen, that happen. Then dream right. All that was, we dream. See all."

After being told what to dream. It was no different than Turtlehead's omens. Hatilshay slumped over his horse, paying no heed to the trail. What did it matter? He came suddenly alert, for if there were no gods, he was alone. He thumped his heels against the horse's sides and caught up with the old one and Turtlehead. Still he was not comforted.

Poor Lo galloped past, waving them to follow. The Yuma knew what a horse was good for. Hatilshay kicked his horse to a gallop. Though he bounced painfully, it was the one day of the journey that Hatilshay enjoyed. For once, the Papago had reason to complain.

"Another day like this," he said when he'd examined the horses, "and they will fall dead beneath us."

"Then we'll eat well," said Hatilshay.

"No fall dead," said Poor Lo. "You here."

Chulito snorted.

"He means we have arrived," explained Hatilshay.

"Yes," said Poor Lo. "Arrived."

"I see no wagons, nor any river."

"Over hill. You see."

The hill was sandier than any they'd crossed. Hatilshay crawled up through the sparse growth and looked down on a ragged band of lights. He could not say if they were small fires that were close or large fires at a distance. The only other thing he could see of the valley was a glint of water. He returned to the shaman.

"You saw no wagons?" asked the old one.

"It is too dark." Hatilshay hoped no one else would go to look.

Turtlehead spoke from the blanket's folds. "The stiffness tells me they are there."

"Buckskin loses its stiffness when it is worked," Hatilshay told him.

"Buckskin can be bent. My legs cannot."

Hatilshay would have said more but he caught the shaman's eye. It was a look that would have stopped a war leader's speech.

"You go now?" suggested Turtlehead.

If this white-eye village was like the other, there would be few places to hide. Dark would give cover but would also make Hatilshay's sight more uncertain. There was also the Yuma, no more to be trusted than Chulito. Less, for Poor Lo was sensible about horses.

"I will go now," Hatilshay decided. It was best to take the enemy by surprise. "The Yuma will guide me."

When he explained to Poor Lo, the Yuma said nothing but "Eat now," becoming more stubborn each time he repeated it. Chulito must have heard for he carried the food bags to the shaman.

"For a favor," he said, dropping them at the old man's feet, "keep the savage from them. Little remains for the journey home."

Poor Lo studied the nearly flat pouches, then grinned at Hatilshay. "We go now. Maybe trade."

"After we make a big bang?" It was the sort of trading Hatilshay approved. Chulito didn't, for he went to tend the horses, muttering about thieves and Yankee vengeance. Hatilshay followed Poor Lo up the hill, feeling easier about leaving camp. A worried Papago was far safer than one who was smug and happy.

They went much farther down the hill than they'd gone up and the downward side was almost as steep as a cliff. It reminded Hatilshay of the dry riverbanks in the desert and when they reached the bottom, he realized it must have been cut the same way.

"Does the river flood often?" Hatilshay asked.

"All time." Then Poor Lo must have understood what he meant and added, "This far in grandfather days. All the same, Yankee crazy live here."

When he saw the village, Hatilshay agreed. Mud-brick buildings, large and small tents and a few unsheltered camps filled the narrow space between high bank and river. A few lights showed up on the bank but if the river flooded and cut away the cliff base, these men would be no safer than those on the shore. It was foolish of the white-eyes to build for the river to take. The ones with tents had more sense, but not much. This was not the sort of place to camp, not at this time of year.

Hatilshay had mistaken lighted doorways for fires. Through them men could be seen and laughter, shouts and strange music heard. One large tent had a wooden floor on which men danced with women, whirling and stomping. Most of the brick buildings were dark. Poor Lo crept around them testing doors and windows. None opened.

"Maybe one time they forget," he said. "Now we trade."

Hatilshay knelt and brushed the ground with his fingers. "Tracks of the wagons!"

"This store. Wagons all the time come."

"Perhaps the carving is here."

"Maybe. Maybe no." Poor Lo moved away. "Come. We trade."

"You trade. I will follow these."

The tracks led behind another brick building, lighted and filled with white-eyes. More than one wagon had stopped there and tracks went from the badly scruffed ground by the door to the next building, around to a tent and also up the steep bank. While Hatilshay decided which to follow, the door of the building opened, almost catching him in the light. He scuttled around the corner and crouched there, listening to the white-eye voices. One broke off, making a surprised noise. As Hatilshay tensed, he heard Poor Lo speak. And in the white-eye tongue! He peered around the corner.

Two white-eyes stood just outside the door, their backs to Hatilshay. One wore the blue coat of a soldier. The other carried a light. That one spoke to Poor Lo, shaking his head. The Yuma glanced around as if looking for Hatilshay, then walked away. The soldier turned to shut the door and Hatilshay saw his face.

Bobcat Whiskers!

Bobcat
Whiskers

The two men walked up along the steep bank. Hatilshay waited until the circle of light was far ahead before he followed. He stopped often to search the ground, always finding wagon tracks near his feet. Once the men spoke directly above him and he feared discovery as the light swung over his head. But the men walked on and Hatilshay soon found that the wagon tracks doubled back to climb the hill. The brick building to which they led was almost directly above the one they'd left.

Monster ground squirrels could have been at work on the hill, for it was covered with holes and piles of dirt. Hatilshay had no trouble finding cover as he crept closer to the two men. The roof of the building came far out in front and was held up by six posts and two people.

Hatilshay squirmed closer, for the white-eye light swung in a way that moved shadows and confused the vision. The six posts had been hastily placed but the two figures stood firmly on white bases and pushed white blocks against the roof. Spirit carvings! Had the wagons brought one to replace each post? Yes, for six cloth-covered bundles lay nearby. Turtlehead would stand gazing over the town while holding up the white-eye's roof. Hatilshay smothered laughter and tried to move closer.

The white-eye with the light showed the standing carvings to Bobcat Whiskers. The first figure wore the blue coat of a soldier and a cap that stuck out at the sides. He had body lice, for his hand scratched inside the coat. The second did not look like a white-eye. His garment came to his knees, much as the Hopi wore theirs, but his chest was covered with a carved shield and both his arms wore bow guards that reached to the elbow. Hatilshay thought he glimpsed guards on the shins, also. The headgear looked like a spirit dancer's crown turned halfway around.

At last the light was placed beside one of the cloth-covered bundles which was then unwrapped. Hatilshay did not need an understanding of the white-eye tongue to know what was said. The light-carrier's tone and gestures spoke plainly.

"Look at this terrible thing," they said. "Who could have done such a terrible thing?

Bobcat Whiskers shook his head as if agreeing it was a terrible thing and behaving as if he'd never seen the carving before, yet Hatilshay clearly saw the red of the medicine blanket. What treachery was Bobcat Whiskers playing on one of his own kind?

As the two men talked, Bobcat Whiskers kept glancing at the sky as if worried about rain. Light Carrier appeared to agree, and they lifted Turtlehead's carving and carried it down the bank, taking the light with them. Hatilshay watched the light move away, then return farther down. He planned to make his way straight down when he was safe from discovery. Then suddenly the clanging of metal sounded from the town.

The two men halted. When the light moved again, it bobbed and joggled. The town lights disappeared as men crowded through tent and building doors. Hatilshay squinted to see what drew them toward the river, then remembered Turtlehead's carving. It was carried into the building below him. The door was scarcely shut before Hatilshay was sliding down the steep bank.

The door wouldn't open. Hatilshay ran around the building in time to see Bobcat Whiskers and some other men leaving through a door that faced the river.

Hearing nothing inside, Hatilshay edged toward the open door. A man shouted and ran toward him, waving his arms. Hatilshay leaped past the door and into the sheltering darkness. He didn't stop running until he came to the place where Poor Lo had led him down the bank. If the Yuma planned to return, this was the reasonable place to meet. Hatilshay turned his face to the wind and decided not to wait. He didn't wish to climb the bank in the rain. A low call stopped him.

The Yuma lurched toward him, a bundle over one shoulder and a large iron pot in his hand. Hatilshay took hold of the handle and gasped. Without help, Poor Lo would not have gotten the pot of stew up the bank. When they staggered over the top, the Yuma gave the bundle to Hatilshay. For its size, it had no weight at all.

"Bread," Poor Lo told him and dipped his fingers into the stew and licked them.

Hatilshay tried to hurry him. "There is rain coming."

"Good. Make more stew."

"Maybe the Yankees come."

"Maybe. Maybe no." But he stopped eating and moved.

Carrying the pot between them was awkward but they managed to walk fast without slopping too much hot liquid over the rim. The Yuma must have taken it right off a white-eye's cook fire. Here was the person to travel with. Not Chulito or even Turtlehead with his signs and evil omens. Poor Lo would never come empty-handed from a raid. He was almost as proud as the Yuma when they set the pot down in front of Chulito and the shaman.

"Good trade." Poor Lo made a hitting motion. "Bang, bang! Everybody run."

"That is not trade," Chulito told him. "You stole this."

"No, make trade. Yankees like run, shoot guns. All the time chase Poor Lo. I give Yankees fun." He scooped meat from the pot. "This time Poor Lo get something."

"You will bring the Yankees on us."

If Poor Lo made an answer, the words could not squeeze past the food stuffed in his mouth.

"Savage!" said Chulito.

He broke off chunks of the soft square bread and dunked them into the stew. His civilized way of eating gave him mostly liquid but it made the meat and vegetables easier for the others to find. No one spoke until stew and bread were gone. Poor Lo draped the red and white bread cloth over his shoulders.

"That cloth is for food," Chulito said. "It is put on a table and food is put on it."

"That is stupid," said Poor Lo. "Get food on it, nobody wear."

While they argued about it, Hatilshay told the shaman and Turtlehead that he had found the spirit carving. He did not speak of the roof or the other carvings, but he said that Bobcat Whiskers had helped to carry it. To his surprise, Turtlehead was not angry that he'd done no more than watch.

"It is good," he said. "Tomorrow you will destroy it and I will be well."

"First we must find a way to take it from the white-eyes," Hatilshay reminded him.

"Sleep and the vision will come."

"Vision!" It was the sort of help only Turtlehead would offer. "It is Poor Lo who dreams, not I."

"The Yuma sees the past. You see what will come." Turtlehead raised himself on one arm. "Did you not see the coming of the white-eye? And you saw the finding of the Yuma where the bells ring."

"I saw no vision of the Yuma and there were no bells."

But Turtlehead had pulled the blanket over his head and turned on his side, leaving Hatilshay to argue with the yellow sun symbol. There was silence until the shaman said quietly, "He believes you are a wise one."

Hatilshay stared at him. It was a name given to one who might some day prove to be a shaman. "I am no healer."

"Not yet."

"Not ever."

The old one smiled. "It is the medicine that chooses the user."

"None will choose me." For he would believe no omen or dream, and how else could a shaman receive his power? Hatilshay remembered the dreams of the Yuma, the ones he dreamed a second time to correct. Perhaps shamans did do their own choosing, for most of the power must be in the belief of the patient.

If the shaman had not opened his medicine pouch to prepare for chanting, Hatilshay might have asked his questions aloud. Instead, he went to watch Chulito and Poor Lo prepare a stick game to decide the ownership of the red and white cloth. They were setting out the ring of counting stones, having agreed to four groups of ten. The first marker to travel twice around the circle would win. They argued over the openings between the groups of ten stones.

"Must go to the four directions," insisted Poor Lo.

"That is a heathen superstition," Chulito told him. "The spaces are for easy counting. It is of no importance where they open."

"Make important if I win."

Chulito moved his stones, taking Poor Lo's spacing as a guide. When the circle was completed, they began cutting twigs for the dice sticks. They fought over the number of sticks and how many points for each. They settled on three sticks, one point for each flat side turned up. Poor Lo demanded first throw of the sticks because the red and white cloth was his. On Chulito's second turn, his marker finished at the same stone as Poor Lo's, sending it back to the beginning. It would be a long game. Hatilshay stretched out to sleep.

The sticks hit the ground, the markers clinked on the stones and between arguments could be heard the shaman's high, thin chant. Each had his place. None of them doubted, not even when they argued different beliefs that could not all be true. Even Chulito, for all his talk of heathen superstition, had placed the openings to the four directions. Did he also believe that playing a stick game in summer would bring a bite from a rattlesnake in punishment? And did such a rule hold true when winter days were warm as early summer, bringing at least one rattler out to sun? He must ask the Yuma if stick games were played only at night in this land. The nights were cold enough to send snakes and lizards to sleep, though not as chill as Hatilshay expected winter nights to be.

Chulito suddenly yelled, "You moved it! It was round side up. Two points only."

"Three," said Poor Lo.

"Two! Thief, cheat, eater of fish!"

"All time talk. Empty gourd make much noise."

A chill gust of wind swept over them, then rain spattered. Poor Lo grabbed the red and white cloth.

"Game over." He scrambled out of Chulito's reach. "We play tomorrow."

The Papago's voice but not the words could be heard over the rain. It was as if the gods had tired of their bickering. But there were no gods, Hatilshay remembered. Just the season for rains. He curled himself as small as possible and endured until the shower passed and he could sleep.

He was the last to waken. Poor Lo was not in camp but his horse stood with Chulito's. The red and white cloth, held down by the counting stones, was spread to dry. The sun rose higher, Chulito finished with the horses and still Poor Lo did not appear.

The shaman sat gazing over the horizon. Turtlehead pushed himself up on one elbow and moaned.

"It is the dampness," Hatilshay told him. "We are all stiff."

"Not stiff to death," said the blanket-wearer. "The white-eye witch is near. He chants over the spirit carving."

Chulito led up the twin horses. His own was saddled. Over Poor Lo's he threw the folded red and white cloth. To stop Turtlehead's complaining, Hatilshay asked the Papago, "Where is Poor Lo?"

"He is gone."

Hatilshay gasped. It was a phrase used for those who died. His chest tightened with grief, grief from knowing there was no spirit mountain to welcome Poor Lo. And from the same knowledge came the knot of fear for himself, which he turned to anger against Chulito.

"So you kill for a horse and a bit of cloth," he shouted. "Is this the teaching of the Yankees? Is this the reason your people put you out of the village?"

"They didn't put me out," Chulito shouted back. "I left!"

"And you think to return as a great warrior. Did you take hairs from the Yuma's head? Give them to me."

Hatilshay drew his knife and moved toward the Papago.

"You are crazy!" Chulito backed into the Yuma's horse. "I knew you were not to be trusted! Apache devil!"

"Give me the scalp," demanded Hatilshay, prodding with the knife point.

"Holy Mary, Mother of God!" Chulito made the sign of the Black Robes and fell to his knees.

"What do you?" asked the old one.

"This one has murdered the Yuma." Hatilshay answered in the tongue the old one had used, the Mexican.

"He has told you this?"

"He said that the . . . ." Hatilshay's face flushed, for the phrase "he is gone" did not have the same meaning in the Mexican nor would the Papago have known the meaning it would carry for one of The People. All the same, it was the sort of thing one would expect a Papago to do. Especially this one, who valued horses above food. Again Hatilshay asked, "Where is Poor Lo?"

Chulito scrooched backward, under the horse's belly, and came up on the side opposite Hatilshay. Over the horse's back, he said, "He is gone to the town. Last night he saw the man he trades with. He must wait for the steamboat."

"But the steamboat is not coming now."

"But this man pays him to wait." Chulito scowled. "He lies, cheats and steals."

"And very well," agreed Hatilshay.

Muttering to himself, Chulito went to lead up the rest of the horses. When he again stood before Hatilshay, he asked, "Will you ask my pardon?"

"For what?"

The Papago motioned nervously at his middle. "For what you did. For what you planned to do. For what you said."

Hatilshay had a thought which pleased him. "Is it the way of the civilized?"

"Yes."

"I will ask pardon of you when Bobcat Whiskers asks pardon of this one." Hatilshay's chin motioned toward the blanket-wearer.

"For what?"

"For making the carving."

"He did not make the carving, stupid one. Only the great carvers in the eastern villages can make those."

"You lie!" Hatilshay did not wait for his protest. "How could they make a carving of one they had never seen?"

"They didn't." Chulito looked as fearful as when Hatilshay had threatened with the knife. He swung onto his horse. "We must go."

Hatilshay grabbed for the reins. "Bobcat Whiskers made the carving."

"No!"

"He did something to the carving and you helped."

"No!" But his look of guilt said he lied.

"I saw," Hatilshay told him.

"You could not. We were in the . . . ." He caught the rest of the words but already he'd said too much.

"I saw," repeated Hatilshay, then remembered the cloth-covered bundles. "Are the other seven carvings of the Indians?"

"Why should a great and rich man want the Indians? They are of the greatest soldiers." Then Chulito's eyes widened and he gasped. "How do you know?"

"I saw."

Now fear was mixed with the Papago's guilt. He pulled a Black Robe medal from under his shirt and clutched it tightly. Then he leaned over to yell at Turtlehead, "They are all of the greatest soldiers and they are dead. All of them dead! Dead!"

With a shriek, the red and yellow blanket stiffened into the shape of the cloth-covered bundles. Furious, Hatilshay stepped in front of the Papago's horse. He folded his arms and stared out at the horizon, trying to unloose his sight the way the shaman did.

"Bobcat Whiskers betrays a Yankee," he said.

"The saints protect me," muttered Chulito.

Hatilshay tried to keep all emotion from his voice.

"He will betray you. There will come a time of darkness. In the darkness you must listen with your heart. Then you will know your friends."

"Devil!" Chulito made his horse rear. Hatilshay leaped backward. As the Papago galloped away, he shouted, "Witch!" It sounded no better from him than it had from Turtlehead.

From under the blanket came, "You are truly a wise one."

"I but frightened him," said Hatilshay. "And not so much that he forgot to take the Yuma's horse. He is running to the white-eyes. We will have trouble with him."

"As you say," murmured Turtlehead. "You see that which will be."

The shaman looked at Hatilshay, his head to one side and his eyes bright, like a roadrunner that has raced and won.

"Let us go," said Hatilshay. And realized he must get Turtlehead, stiffened more than ever by Chulito's outburst, on the horse by himself.

"Only a Papago would think of such sly revenge," he muttered. "And he took the Yuma's horse. How do I know he did not kill Poor Lo?"

No one reassured him and an uneasy feeling grew in his stomach.

"Let us go," he said wearily.

The Iron Ring

Hatilshay stooped to put his shoulder under Turtle-head's rump. He pushed while the shaman pulled on the blanket-wearer's arms until they finally had Turtle-head belly down over the horse. Hatilshay stepped back, willing to let him ride that way. But the shaman seized one leg and tugged it over the horse's back, ignoring the cries of pain. When he had his nephew properly seated, the old one mounted his own horse. Though his back was still straight, he moved as if under a great weight. The weight of many years, Hatilshay realized sadly. And his heart ached for one who would soon be gone forever.

Hatilshay led his horse. He was more comfortable on his own feet and it was easier to look for the trail. Horses could not use the one Poor Lo had shown him the night before but he found wagon tracks farther upriver. They led back and forth down the steep hill, past broken wagons and two dead horses. At the base of the hill, there was little space between the river and huge piles of dirt. The bank had not fallen. The dirt came from caves and tunnels dug into the hillside. Ditches and holes had been dug at the edge of the river and even in the shallow water. Everywhere were broken boards, bottles, dead campfires and muddy tatters of cloth.

"What do they hunt?" asked Turtlehead.

"Gold," said his uncle.

The blanket-wearer turned to watch two men shoveling dirt into a long wooden trough where water washed most of it into the river. "They work hard. Is it a powerful charm?"

The shaman slid from his horse and handed the reins to Hatilshay. "That cave appears deserted. Put the horses there. We will take only my nephew's into the village."

Hatilshay obeyed, noting the landmarks carefully. They went openly to the village, following the wagon tracks. There was no other place to walk unless they wished to climb the dirt hills or wade through ditches. At the edge of the town, six men carried a platform with a tent on it to higher ground. Groups of white-eyes talked, eyes darting from sky to river to buildings. Hatilshay snorted. Didn't they know it was not so much the rain that fell here as the rain from the mountains that flooded rivers? The water must have risen during the night, but flood height for this season should be almost reached by now. Hatilshay remembered what Poor Lo had said about high floods. In his grandfather's day, he'd said. They might not come again until his grandchildren's day but come they would and then even the house with the spirit carvings would be carried down river. Foolish white-eyes! A brush wickiup took little time to build and the river was welcome to it, if one was foolish enough to camp where the river could reach it.

The shaman spoke softly. "Where is the spirit carving hidden?"

Hatilshay led them around behind the mud-brick buildings, glad to be hidden from the white-eyes. Many had turned to stare and mutter. All the buildings were open. Men came and went through the doors Poor Lo had tried to open the night before. Most of the wagon tracks had been washed away in the rain.

"In that one." But Hatilshay was not certain it was the same building Bobcat Whiskers had come from.

"I do not see the carving," said Turtlehead.

"Do you see through walls?" asked Hatilshay.

"The door is open."

Without light inside the building, Hatilshay had not been able to tell. Hoping Turtlehead would tell him more, he said, "The door gives a small view."

There was silence until Hatilshay realized they were waiting for him to speak or take action. He felt tired, a weariness that rest would not help. It came not from the journey but from the decisions forced upon him. Why did the old one leave them in his hands? Hatilshay pushed down his anger. The shaman was old, with many years of weariness to carry. Again Hatilshay felt the pang of sorrow when thinking of the old one.

"I will look," Hatilshay told him.

There were no white-eyes in sight. It should be as easy as stalking game. He approached the open door in the same manner, circling to come upon it from the side. In the center of barrels and cases of bottles stood the carving. A thin coating of white paint did not hide the red of the blanket. Lighter places showed the markings and sun symbol.

"Hey!" A white-eye with hair the color of flames came from the front part of the building, yelling first at Hatilshay, then over his shoulder.

Hatilshay backed away, feeling behind him for the door. He feared to turn his back on the man. Just as his fingers found the edge of the doorway, the man who'd carried the light the night before came up behind Fire Head. He also shouted, but Hatilshay slid around the doorway and ran. Not toward the shaman and Turtlehead, but for cover in the opposite direction. The door slammed after him. When he was safe behind a mound of dirt, he sank to the ground.

He was tired of chasing Turtlehead's carving and in turn being chased by white-eyes. All because of the blanket-wearer's strong belief in omens, signs and powers. "Heathen superstitions" Chulito had called them and he was right. But the Papago also had strange notions. Did the white-eyes have them too? Hatilshay shook his head. These thoughts would not steal the carving from the white-eyes.

A bottle lay near his foot. On it was a drawing much like Bobcat Whiskers' but colored brighter than life. A white-eye stood in a forest, one foot resting on a large stump. If the man wore the blue of a soldier, Hatilshay might scratch whiskers on him with charcoal and convince Turtlehead he'd worked a spell against the spirit carver.

He kicked the bottle aside. Such a thing would give Turtlehead the pleasure of revenge but would not lessen the stiffness in his body. The carving must be stolen and destroyed. Wearily Hatilshay got to his feet and returned to where the shaman crouched beside the horse bearing his nephew.

"It is there," Hatilshay told them.

"We must wait for the white-eyes to leave?" The shaman made it a question.

"They fasten the doors when they leave. The Yuma tried them last night. They could not be opened." Hatilshay thought back to the night before. "The Yuma made a noise that sent the white-eyes running from the buildings. That is when he stole the food."

"We will make the noise."

"I do not know how."

Turtlehead groaned as he shifted on the horse's back. "I grow fast to this animal. Ask the Yuma."

The shaman asked Hatilshay, "Do you know where he trades?"

Turtlehead answered. "I saw him."

He slapped the horse, turning it between the buildings toward the river and the main trail. Hatilshay followed with the shaman. They found Poor Lo sitting against the building where he'd first tried the doors and windows. Store, he'd called it. The Yuma was so near the color of the mud bricks that Hatilshay wondered how Turtlehead had seen him when they entered the village.

"I see you again," Hatilshay told the Yuma. "I feared the Papago had sent you to the spirit mountain."

"That one." Poor Lo's tone dismissed Chulito as one of no importance.

"What do you?" asked Hatilshay.

"Poor Lo trade. Sit for Yankee, wait for steamboat."

"But the steamboat will not come soon."

"I know that. You know that. Yankee not know that maybe two, three days."

"When he knows, the Yankee will be very angry."

"All the same, Poor Lo eat good two, three days."

Hatilshay settled beside the Yuma, his back against the rough wall. The shaman crouched beside him. Turtlehead remained on his horse. From the way he drew the blanket around him, he felt as exposed to the white-eyes as Hatilshay did. A wall at one's back helped.

There was more talk of trading, the sort Poor Lo did, of the rising river, which Poor Lo agreed had reached peak flood for this season, of stealing horses from the wagons, which Poor Lo said had left on their return journey, and of the evilness of the Yankees. At last the courtesies were finished and Hatilshay could ask about the noise.

Poor Lo explained that an iron ring hung from a tree near the river. When struck by an iron bar hanging beside it, all Yankees ran as if summoned by a war leader.

"Is it a fighting signal?" asked the shaman.

Poor Lo looked confused. "Sometime soldier come."

The old one frowned. "I do not like them to think it is war."

"No war, come! Steamboat whistle." Poor Lo let out a shriek that made all the white-eyes jump and stare. The Yuma ignored them. "Hit iron, all come. River flood, hit iron, all come."

Poor Lo laughed. "Little dog on tree in river, hit iron, all come. Yankee swim out, dog bite! Still in river, maybe."

Turtlehead grumbled in their own tongue, "I will put this one in the river to stop his talk. Tell him to strike the iron."

Hatilshay asked. Poor Lo shook his head.

"Must sit," he kept saying.

"The blanket-wearer can sit for you," said Hatilshay. It was all Turtlehead could do anyway.

"No. Steamboat come, all run here." Poor Lo waved to a closed window over his head. "Poor Lo jump quick, be first. That one not jump quick."

"But the steamboat is not coming," Hatilshay reminded him.

"Steamboat come some day." Poor Lo brightened. "Maybe come one day, two. Who can say? But come some day."

"But it will not come today."

"Maybe, maybe no." The Yuma looked at the sun.

"Yankee bring food soon. Poor Lo sit all day, want food."

"It is no matter," Hatilshay told him. If Turtlehead could not sit and wait for the white-eye's magic writing, he could sit beside the iron ring. In their own tongue, to be certain that Turtlehead understood, Hatilshay told the shaman, "Two are needed to carry the spirit carving. I saw that last night. If you strike the iron, who is to help me carry?"

The shaman did not answer. The question was not for him. They waited so long that Hatilshay wondered if he'd spoken loudly enough for Turtlehead to hear. Surely he had wit enough to think it out. It was no more difficult than some of the omens he read. Omens! Did the blanket-wearer wait for an omen? If so, Hatilshay would give him one.

"When I ran from the white-eye place, I saw a man standing beside a tree. He stood on one leg. That one was stiff but the other was bent. Beneath the bent leg there formed the trunk of a tree." Fearing Turtlehead might read the wrong meaning into it, Hatilshay added, "It was as if the stiffness poured from his leg."

"This was a vision?" asked Turtlehead.

"It is what I saw." Hatilshay hoped he'd been hidden from Turtlehead's view when he inspected the bottle.

"I will strike the iron," said Turtlehead.

Hatilshay let out his breath. The shaman met his eyes and the laugh wrinkles deepened.

"Where you go?" asked Poor Lo.

"We go to trade," Hatilshay told him.

They followed the river bank until they found the circle of heavy iron.

"You did not see this in your vision?" asked Turtlehead.

"No, only trees."

"These trees?"

Hatilshay choked back a lie. Turtlehead must have heard it as a sound of anger for his voice turned meek as a child's.

"I wish only to know if the stiffness leaves before or after striking the iron."

"My vision is not certain on distance." He led the horse past the iron ring and into a patch of bushes. "White-eyes may be watching."

The shaman agreed. "Wait here until you strike the ring."

That would be done at sunset, which was not far away. Turtlehead would then ride to the cave where they'd left the other two horses. After Hatilshay and the shaman joined him, the spirit carving would be destroyed. The old one did not say what Turtlehead should do if he and Hatilshay were caught and never arrived at the cave. Perhaps, like Hatilshay, he did not care to think about it.

Hatilshay and the shaman crept around the town, through torn land and small camps. Twice they saw men sitting with guns across their knees, guarding a hole in the ground. Hatilshay wondered if they would run when the iron ring was struck.

He led the old one to the place where he'd rested

after fleeing from the brick building. They settled on their heels to wait, for it was still light. Light enough for the shaman to find the bottle. Hatilshay watched him examine the drawing. At last the old one spoke.

"The Papago will tell you that a weeded field bears stronger corn. It would seem to be true also of visions."

"Would you have me tell him the man I saw was a white-eye?" Hatilshay's hand gestured. "No matter. There was no vision, not now or ever."

He told it all, from mistaking the yucca for a white-eye soldier to using the drawing on the bottle to move Turtlehead.

"Now you know," he finished. "There were no visions. Only eyes that do not see true and a quick tongue."

"Do you forget that I named you?" said the shaman. "I have known of your false vision since you stood at my shoulder to hear the legends of the stars. Do you think it is by chance you received those eyes? Giver-of-Life does nothing without reason."

"There is no Giver-of-Life." Hatilshay held his body stiff, prepared for the shaman's anger.

The old one said only, "And in what vision was this revealed?"

"I need no vision." Hatilshay almost shouted it. "I need only reason."

"And your reason tells you there is no Giver-of-Life. Have you taken the god of the Black Robes, then?"

"That is it! You have heard the Papago talk of

the Black Robes and their god. The Yuma talks of his god and the spirit mountain."

"They agree."

"They argue! You have heard them. They cannot both be right. And if one of them is right, The People are also wrong."

Quietly the shaman asked, "When you hunt, do you think hard about the game you seek?"

Hatilshay almost groaned aloud. Ask the shaman about the gods and he speaks of hunting. Hatilshay should have expected no more. All the same, he answered. "Everyone knows that thoughts of the game will alert it and it will flee."

"Those who hunt the buffalo say that thinking hard about the game draws it to the hunter."

"They are wrong."

"Right or wrong is of no importance," said the old one. "What matters is that you and the buffalo hunters agree."

"We do not agree!" Had the shaman lost his wits? "We would argue." Silently the thought continued, just as Poor Lo and Chulito argue.

Quietly the shaman said, "Then you agree. For you could not argue if you did not agree that thoughts have power over game. That is a matter of great importance."

Yes, it was true. Chulito and Poor Lo both claimed a god made the earth. They only argued about which god and how the earth was made. So, too, with The People. And with the Hopi, from what he'd heard.

"It will take much thinking on," said Hatilshay.

"You give thanks to Giver-of-Life." With that statement, the shaman left the subject, returning to Hatilshay's visions. "You thought the yucca to be a man. You had never seen a white-eye nor did you know that white-eye soldiers were in our land. Why then did you not say a Mexican was there, or a Papago? Both use that trail."

"It was white-eye that came first to my tongue."

"Yes." The shaman smiled. "Against all reason. Just as it was against reason to tell my nephew you heard bells when he searched for omens."

Before Hatilshay could answer, iron clanged against iron. They scrambled over the dirt pile. White-eyes ran as they had the night before but not so many from the buildings and tents. Hoping the ones sliding down the hillside would not notice them, Hatilshay followed the old one to the door of the building. What if it did not open?

It did. And the room beyond was empty of white-eyes. Hatilshay dragged at the carving's head while the old one lifted the square base. They staggered out the door and across the long open space behind the buildings. When they reached cover, the shaman dropped his end. They both panted.

"No sound of horse," gasped Hatilshay. "He should come this way."

"He may hide. Come later." The old one leaned against the carving. "Rest."

When they moved on, the shaman led, setting an easy pace. The carving seemed lighter to Hatilshay. He

laughed. A successful raid, though it was not the one
he and Turtlehead had started on. Hatilshay hadn't felt
this tall since bringing his mother the first rabbits he'd
shot. His pride had fallen quickly under the jokes of
his friends, for he'd been a poor marksman and a long
time in bringing down his first game. But this victory
would last and be told for many winters. Who else
could steal a wooden Turtlehead from the white-eyes?

Though it was full dark, the shaman found the cave
without trouble. They crowded past the two horses and
set the carving on the packed dirt. Hatilshay gathered
what few twigs remained on the hillside. The fire was
small and short lived but they had time enough to inspect the carving.

"It is a Hopi!" said Hatilshay.

The red and yellow paint had hidden the true carving as surely as a real blanket. Now that a thin layer
of white covered it all, he could see the figure wore
skirt and cloak like a Hopi. What had looked like folds
of red blanket over the forehead was really a wreath
of leaves, the sort of thing a Hopi might wear for
ceremonies. But the face was white-eye.

"No," he corrected himself. "Not Hopi."

"And not my nephew." Quickly the shaman added,
"Still, it must be destroyed. My nephew will say it
can be changed back again."

"That is true. One needs only red paint."

The old one's voice was sad. "The blanket is not
my nephew, though now even he believes it is."

Hatilshay could not resist the chance to place blame,

though only indirectly. "He was told the blanket had great power," he said.

"He was told only that it came from far to the east, where the sun rose from salty water. The power he saw for himself in the symbols." After a hesitation, the old one added, "His vision is false."

"Then he should be the wise one."

"False vision is not necessary for a shaman. It may be enough that he travel among strange people, learning the plants that will heal wounds, purge a man or ease his pain. This shaman, if he has listened as he traveled, learns much of the nature of men. He knows men wound themselves, invisible wounds that can be cured only by loud and visible ceremony."

"Like your nephew." Though he could not see, Hatilshay was certain the shaman nodded. "It is as I thought. All talk of power is a lie."

"No," said the old one quickly. "All things have power, each according to its nature. My nephew's blanket gives courage to my nephew but even an ordinary blanket has power to hold back the cold. That, too, is a wondrous thing. Only remember, the blanket does not keep one warm unless it is used."

Hatilshay pondered that, watching the horses outlined against the sky. When their heads turned and one whickered, Hatilshay said, "Your nephew comes."

But it was Poor Lo who called, "No shoot! Friend."

He sent the horse in first, then crept through the entrance close to the wall. Hatilshay wondered what cause the Yuma had to fear them.

"You bring my nephew's horse," said the shaman. "Where is the rider?"

Hatilshay had seen nothing to identify the horse. Truly his eyes were weak, too weak for raiding. He only half heard Poor Lo's offer to trade.

"You trade with the Yankee and must sit by his house," said the shaman.

"Sit only by day. Boat not go at night. You have food?"

"The Papago has the food."

"Have horses. Eat horse?"

"The horses are also the Papago's."

Poor Lo sighed heavily. "Too sad. No food, no trade. All the same, I tell you. Soldiers take Red Blanket. Hang maybe."

Poor Lo's War

Poor Lo kept repeating that he was not to blame. They had not told him what they planned. That was true. Hatilshay remembered speaking in the tongue of The People so that Turtlehead would understand clearly. The Yuma, if he had known, would have warned them to run after hitting the iron ring.

"Red blanket hit, not run. Stand one leg, like bird. Why stand one leg?"

"Perhaps he saw a water bird," said Hatilshay. The grief he'd felt that morning when he thought the Yuma gone was only a shadow of what he felt now. "The blame is mine."

"Not every ceremony heals," said the shaman.

"No ceremony will take your nephew from the Yankees. No vision, either."

Poor Lo spoke. "We fight soldiers?" He sounded happy at the thought.

"The Yankees guard their camp well," Hatilshay told him. "I do not think we can sneak in, even at night."

"Not sneak, fight! Like old wars. Take bows, war clubs. Stand in line. Call soldiers come fight!"

"They will kill us."

"Go spirit mountain all the same. This way, much honor."

"This way, much crazy. No man fights just to be killed."

"Yes, that why fight war."

"War is for raiding, to get food and supplies." No man of The People fought to the death unless trapped or defending his family. "If all the men are killed, who will care for the wives and children? They will starve."

"Go spirit mountain all the same."

Chulito was right; the Yuma was a savage. "We will fight the soldiers in the way of my people. We will scout the camp at daylight, then sneak in to rescue the Red Blanket."

"Sneak." Poor Lo's voice had the same tone as Chulito's when he called The People uncivilized. "Your people not men."

Hatilshay crept past the horses to the mouth of the cave. He huddled there, dozing fitfully in spite of the cold and hunger, until the eastern sky paled. The horses crowded past him, taking themselves to water.

"Should I go after them?" Hatilshay asked the shaman, then repeated it in Mexican so that Poor Lo could understand.

"No," said the old one. "Perhaps they will stay near."

"Yankees take," said Poor Lo. "Yankees big thieves."

He bent over the spirit carving, poked it with his toe and grinned at the shaman. "You trade with Yankees?"

The old one moved to the entrance and sprinkled sacred pollen to the four directions. After gazing in silence at the rising sun, he turned toward the white-eye village and chose a careful way down the hillside. Hatilshay and Poor Lo followed. The Yuma glanced once over his shoulder at the carving.

"Big trade, maybe," he said.

Hatilshay feared that at the first chance the Yuma would return and steal the carving. As they hurried after the shaman, Hatilshay told Poor Lo the story of the carving and Turtlehead's stiffness. He doubted if it would change the Yuma's plan to trade, if he had one, but Poor Lo had told them of Turtlehead's capture, knowing he'd receive nothing in exchange. Perhaps he would help again. But when they settled at the Yuma's place of trade, Hatilshay's hopes vanished. The man who brought Poor Lo a basket of food was the one who had carried the light for Bobcat Whiskers.

As he spoke to the Yuma, he watched Hatilshay and the shaman. At last he returned to the building from which they'd taken the spirit carving, entering by the door facing the river.

"He is angry," guessed Hatilshay.

"Say Poor Lo come too soon. All the time, think Poor Lo lie."

The Yuma gave them each a chunk of bread and a slab of greasy meat. Hatilshay did not remind him that the white-eye was correct. When they finished eating and Poor Lo had licked the inside of the shallow basket, the shaman received his instructions.

"Steamboat come, you jump. Jump there." He pointed at a closed window over their heads. "Jump much quick. Steamboat come, Yankees come. Tens of Yankees, many tens of Yankees. All run there." Again he pointed at the window.

The Yuma fumbled in his rags for two bits of dirty paper which he gave the shaman.

"Writing?" asked Hatilshay.

"Name of Yankee, name of two Yankees," the Yuma explained quickly. Motioning to the window, he said, "Long time, maybe, that open. You give these, get mail."

Again Hatilshay interrupted. "What is mail?"

"Who can know? Make Yankees crazy. You see." He acted out yelling, dancing, pushing, crying. Then he crouched beside the old one. "Put mail in basket. Take there."

He meant the place where the carving had been.

"I give it to the man who brought the food," said the shaman.

Poor Lo drew back and stared. "How you know?"

"It is well known that he has great power," said Hatilshay. "He will chant for us and no soldier will do us harm."

"Truth?" whispered Poor Lo.

The shaman looked hard at Hatilshay but spoke no rebuke. He then turned his gaze to the far horizon and began to chant. His words followed Poor Lo and Hatilshay, so faint that Hatilshay was certain he'd heard false.

"The young know all and are ignorant.
The old know nothing and are wise."

It made no sense. But if Poor Lo was ignorant of its meaning, it might keep him from sneaking off to do some trading.

The army camp was not far from the town. Hatilshay remembered how the soldiers had camped apart from the wagons. At the other white-eye town, the soldiers had been across the river. They must be a different people from other white-eyes. If this was so, there must be many different kinds, just as there were The People, the Hopi, the Navajo, Papago and Yuma. This was something no one had suspected and Hatilshay was certain it was of great importance. Which of the white-eyes were the real ones?

"No Red Blanket," said Poor Lo. "They hang him, maybe. Too sad. Spirit not get out."

Hatilshay squinted down at the camp. "I see no tree big enough for hanging."

"They shoot, maybe."

"We heard no shots."

"They keep, shoot later."

It was the first sensible thing Poor Lo had said. Hatilshay settled himself to watch the tents. The large ones had sides of mud bricks. But the walls were not high and the cloth roofs could be slit. He had only to discover which one held Turtlehead. Three of the largest were guarded. Poor Lo was certain one was the house of the war leader. The other two were together near the center of the camp. Hatilshay could see no way of reaching them without meeting tens of soldiers. Blue uniforms were everywhere, from the river to the horse pens, from one guard line to the other.

"We must draw them away," said Hatilshay.

"We fight?" suggested Poor Lo.

"You fight; I'll sneak."

Poor Lo slid down the rise and walked toward the white-eye guards. Hatilshay gaped at him, too surprised to take advantage of the distraction. He hadn't thought the Yuma would take him seriously. But the fool was brandishing a short knife and shouting at the soldiers in his own tongue. Around the camp, blue-coated men moved toward Poor Lo. Hatilshay forced himself into action. If the Yuma wished to have himself killed, that was his concern. Hatilshay would not waste the chance to rescue Turtlehead.

His only cover was close to the ground. He couldn't raise his head until he was almost to the guard line. Poor Lo still pranced and shouted his challenge, but the white-eyes laughed at him. Worst of all, though their attention was on the Yuma, the guards had not stopped their pacing. There was a chance he could slip into the camp but Hatilshay did not like the odds. He hadn't Poor Lo's faith in the spirit mountain. And when he thought about it, he wasn't even certain Turtlehead was inside the camp. He would lose his life for no more reason than the crazy Yuma. He decided on a quiet retreat. Then Bobcat Whiskers appeared, carrying a stool and drawing tools.

Hatilshay remembered the paper he still carried in his moccasin. He dug it out. Which of the scratches was the name of the long eye and which was the captain's? No matter. The guards would know.

Now Poor Lo shouted at Bobcat Whiskers. He seemed to have called peace in order to trade. And he'd said The People were not true men! Though disgusted, Hatilshay resisted the impulse to make a foolish show of his own courage. He squirmed toward the camp, behind a guard who was grinning and shaking his head over the bargaining between Bobcat Whiskers and Poor Lo. The packed earth of the trail worn by the guards was under his nose, then he was past it. A glance back at the guard, a few more wriggles and he raised his head to find the nearest cover. A hand seized his arm and jerked him to his feet.

Hatilshay looked into a red face with brown spots over the nose and cheeks. His wonder at them almost caused him to forget the paper clutched in his hand. He thrust it at the guard but refused to let it go. Hatilshay knew from experience how quickly such marks disappeared. The guard pushed Hatilshay toward a passing soldier who took him farther into the camp and hailed another blue-uniformed man. This one appeared to understand the marks for he looked closely at them, then questioned Hatilshay, who kept his face clear of expression and said nothing. But his thoughts whirled.

Turtlehead had been right to claim great power for the marks, though the shaman's nephew could never understand the kind of power. Hatilshay was beginning to guess. He knew if he found the captain and drew a picture of Turtlehead's medicine blanket, the captain would understand that Hatilshay sought the wearer. But he would not know why Hatilshay sought him or what help he needed. Hatilshay suspected white-eye marks could tell this and much more.

He came from his thoughts to find the soldier speaking with Bobcat Whiskers. Hatilshay knew he was recognized but there was no anger in the man's eyes. He looked at the paper in Hatilshay's hand and grinned. His eyes laughed, too, as he scrawled more black marks on the paper and waved Hatilshay toward one of the two tent buildings. Hatilshay backed away.

Turtlehead had called the man a witch. Hatilshay knew that was wrong, yet there was something about Bobcat Whiskers that caused uneasiness. His laughter was too much like the jeering Hatilshay remembered from his childhood. He was a trickster, the sort whose jokes would not be funny to everyone. As Hatilshay hurried toward the tent building, he realized that painting the carving had been such a joke. A joke for Bobcat Whiskers and revenge for the Papago. Chulito had been jealous of the captain's interest in two of The People. Knowing the nature of Bobcat Whiskers and something of Turtlehead's fears, Chulito must have suggested painting the carving with a red blanket. Why hadn't Hatilshay seen the spirit carving for what it was?

Turtlehead hadn't, but he was blind to all but omens. And the truth was not to be seen with eyes. What Hatilshay had was an inner vision, a knowing. The old one had it also. Though he claimed his knowledge of men and the ways to heal them came from his travels in far places, Hatilshay was certain the old one had the same inner knowing. How else could he know when a man could be healed only by long ceremony and when an herb was needed?

Where did this knowledge of truth grow and why did only Hatilshay and the old one, of all their village, have it? Was this what the shaman had meant when he said Giver-of-Life did nothing by chance? Had his false-eye vision been given him so the inner one would grow? If so, for what purpose was the inner vision? Uneasiness grew between his ribs. He walked quickly to escape it.

Guards stopped him at the door to the walled tent. Hatilshay refused to give them the paper but turned it as they directed. One guard shouted to someone inside the tent where Hatilshay glimpsed stacks of bundles and boxes. Were white-eyes such thieves that they must guard their possessions? What if the other tent held only boxes?

A guard tugged at the paper, making it clear he must have it in return for what was being passed from inside the tent. Hatilshay feared another of Bobcat Whiskers' jokes, then his heart leaped and he released the paper gladly. Into his hands came the long eye.

He looked downward, afraid his joy would show.

Trying not to clutch his prize too closely, he turned toward the other tent building. The guard who had given him the long eye called out and waved him back the way he'd come. Hatilshay glanced at the other tent. It was so close that if he'd spoken to the guards, Turtlehead might have heard him.

The guard waved again, this time with his long gun. Hatilshay obeyed, but slowly. As he walked, he raised his voice in a chant of trickster coyote. A voice answered, in a different rhythm and so faint Hatilshay could not hear the words. He dragged his feet even more.

He dared not leave the camp. He'd never again get past the guards. Perhaps the Yuma could again draw the attention of the soldiers. Or had he returned to wait for the steamboat that the white-eyes . . . Hatilshay's thoughts leaped from one of Poor Lo's stories to another. He killed a wish to offer hoddentin to the four directions. No prayer could change words already said. If the Yuma had spoken the truth, Hatilshay might yet rescue Turtlehead.

He raised the long eye, lowered it and shuffled backward to the tents, as if seeking a better vantage point. The guard motioned him on, but tiredly.

Again Hatilshay peered through the long eye. He marveled at its power. On a snag drifting in the river he saw a ground squirrel grooming its fur and peering curiously around. Turtlehead would read a meaning in it but Hatilshay saw only a ground squirrel waiting for the snag to run aground.

Turning the long eye downriver, Hatilshay sought a distant view of water. He could not pretend one for he did not know how far the white-eyes could see without long eyes. He found an opening in the trees. Imitating Poor Lo, he pointed, jerked his free hand down in a pulling motion and screeched in the voice of the steamboat.

There were shouts behind him. He glanced back. The guards crowded to the door of the storage tent for long eyes. As soon as they peered through them, Hatilshay whirled, ran to the tent holding the chanter and scrambled to the top of the low brick wall. He drew his knife and slit the tent roofing. A round face peered up at him.

"Chulito! What do you here?"

"I am a prisoner." He looked as if he would weep.

"And the blanket-wearer?"

"I will tell you. Come down." He tugged at Hatilshay's sleeve. "Come! Do you wish the soldiers to find you?"

Not until he'd slipped through the tent roof did Hatilshay realize the soldiers had no need to find him. He was already inside the guard tent of the prisoners.

A Thieving Savage

"A trap," cried Hatilshay.

Chulito moved away, his arm raised in defense. "You cut my tongue and you will never hear of the heathen."

Hatilshay had forgotten the knife in his hand. Perhaps he was not fully a prisoner. He advanced on the Papago. "Silence is better than a lie."

"No lies! I swear by the saints . . . by the blood of the martyrs . . . by the old man on the sacred mountain."

The last convinced Hatilshay he would hear the truth. The Papago might risk the unknown anger of a new god, but the temper of the old god was well known. With a grunt, Hatilshay settled on the dirt floor. Chulito plunked down opposite.

"It is a belief of the Apache devils that one cannot ride horses into a Yankee town," he began. "One must walk and risk meeting with thieving savages. Even when taking refuge in a church, one meets them."

Hatilshay sighed. If the Papago began with finding the Yuma, it would be a very long story.

Chulito continued. "I agreed to care for the Yuma's horse, for he, too, believes one cannot ride a horse into a Yankee town. But the Yuma has reason. Then you drove me from the camp with a heathen curse."

Chulito droned on, telling every step of his search for a horse trail down the steep bank. At last he came to the meeting with Yankee soldiers.

"I told them the one horse had been given me by the great man in Washington. They did not believe. They said horses had been stolen near Fort Yuma and the red cloth had been stolen the night before. They took me for a thief." Chulito thumped his chest. "Do I appear to be a thieving savage?"

"You look like a Papago." To Hatilshay it was the same thing. "Did you not ask for the captain?"

"He rode with the wagon guards. He will return soon, they say. The colonel remained at Fort Yuma. There is no one who can say they know that the horse is mine."

"Bobcat Whiskers? The one who painted the carving."

"You know that he painted it? It was a joke. He is always thinking of jokes."

"He did not think of this one. Only you could have told him of the blanket-wearer's fear."

"It is a heathen superstition. Who would think it could make him ill? I swear that I meant no harm. It was a sin. I know that now. He suffered much during the night."

"He was here?"

"Yes, but I have not yet come to that."

Hatilshay spoke too quickly for the Papago to return to his long story. "Did the soldiers take him for a thief?"

"No, he was brought here to save him. The men in the town were very angry with him. The night before the alarm had called them. While they answered, the town was raided by thieves."

Hatilshay snorted. One pot of stew and some bread wrapped in a cloth. He would like to show them a true raid.

"The one you call Bobcat Whiskers was in the town. He knew the blanket-wearer. Fearing the town men would harm him, he had the soldiers bring him here."

"Why did you not ask Bobcat Whiskers to help you?"

Chulito squirmed.

"You did!" Hatilshay scented the truth. "You asked but he would not help you."

"He said that he can swear one horse is mine, but what of the other? Also, he thinks it will be very funny for the captain to find me here. I begin to believe Poor Lo. The Yankees do not like us. Some of them, that is."

Hatilshay returned to important matters. "What of the blanket-wearer?"

"All the night, he suffered. He moaned and his breath came hard. In the morning, he would not eat and he looked very . . . ." Chulito made a helpless gesture. "I feared for him. But the captain was not here. I asked the guards to bring another officer. He leads the prayers and holy songs though he wears no robe and does not know all the ceremonies of a priest."

"You gave the blanket-wearer to *him?*"

"He is a good man. He may be able to help. And there was no one else."

Chulito repeated his fears for Turtlehead and his sorrow that he'd brought this sickness. Hatilshay believed him. The Papago had been the captain's pet dog and the newcomers had made him jealous. He'd meant only to frighten them away. But sitting with Turtlehead through the night had frightened Chulito.

"It was a sin," he moaned. "I must do great penance."

After the word was explained to him, Hatilshay said, "You can do it by getting the blanket-wearer from the Black Robe."

"He is not yet a priest." Chulito looked puzzled. "Perhaps he may never be."

"It is all the same."

Turtlehead had a nose for magic. He'd smell Black Robe if the man was naked. His meeting with Bobcat Whiskers must have already frightened him near to death. Having a white-eye shaman chanting over him would surely kill him.

Hatilshay rose. "We must get out of here."

"It is time to eat." Chulito leaned back, away from Hatilshay's threatening knife. "The guards bring the food. Better to wait until they have gone."

There was sense to that. "But they will ask how I came here."

"They will think the blanket-wearer was returned. The guards have been changed twice since he was taken and the guards think all Indians look the same."

It could still be a trap. Before Hatilshay could decide, voices and rattling pans sounded outside. He sat down quickly.

"Hide those," whispered Chulito.

Hatilshay slid the long eye under a fold of his loincloth. The knife he slid in his moccasin top but sat with his hand on his leg, fingers at the handle. The door opened. One soldier, gun ready, stepped inside and glanced around. He stood aside while another placed two tin plates and a can of water on the floor. They left and the door swung shut.

Chulito's grin said I told you so. Hatilshay noticed there were no eating tools on the pans, only bread. He ate and drank quickly. Chulito put the empty pans on two others stacked near the door. Hatilshay searched for the slit in the roof. The canvas was stretched so tight it was hard to see. Chulito pointed it out.

"Down." Hatilshay motioned to the Papago. "I must stand on your back to see out. When I am out and on the brick wall, I will reach in for you."

"Why must you stand on my back? I can see as well as you."

Probably better. The thought stung Hatilshay. He held up the long eye. "I have this."

"I can use it."

"I also have a knife."

"That is your answer to everything. Savage!" Chulito bent and put his hands on his knees. "I do this only because of my soul. I must do penance before I die."

"You talk always of sickness and death."

"*I?*" He straightened; Hatilshay pushed him back down. Chulito muttered something in his own tongue about the Apache.

Hatilshay grinned, put one foot on the Papago's thigh and climbed onto the broad back. Chulito grunted. Holding his breath, Hatilshay peered through the slit with one eye, then pushed through to his nose. The space between the two walled tents was empty, but farther away soldiers moved. They walked all together in rows, first one way, then another.

From below, Chulito whispered, "What do you see?"

"They have buried someone and are trampling back and forth over the grave."

"Stupid! They are marching. I can hear the calls. I said that I should look."

"Do not move!"

"Do not waste time. I am not a horse." But he steadied beneath Hatilshay's feet. "Half-starved Apache the captain called him. Hah!"

Hatilshay started to answer, then raised the long eye. It caught in the slit and he jerked to free it.

"Stop that," Chulito warned. "You will push me over."

"Soldiers come, on horses."

"Is it the captain?"

Hatilshay fought to keep his footing on the jiggling back. He gasped, unable to believe the long eye.

"Let me see!" Chulito reared, grabbed for the long eye. Hatilshay yelled and clutched at the roof. With a loud tear, they tumbled to the floor, fighting and kicking the heavy canvas that came down on top. A foot caught Hatilshay in the ribs and a fist bruised his cheekbone. When he got his head clear, the door was open. Two guards stood just inside, guns pointed and their mouths open.

Shouting in the white-eye tongue, Chulito scuttled over the torn canvas on his hands and knees. He was almost between the guards when they caught his shoulders, but he knelt with his head out the door, yelling loud enough to be heard in the town. Hatilshay sat and waited, too bewildered to call. The shaman had ridden in with the captain.

14

Shaman, Mud and Yankee Medicine

Though Chulito spoke the white-eye tongue, Hatilshay followed the story by watching the captain's face. He looked from Hatilshay to Turtlehead with a smile of pity. Then his gaze on Chulito turned to dark anger which faded as the journey through the desert was told. When the Yuma was mentioned, the captain interrupted with questions. He interrupted at other times, too. Chulito must have come to his capture as a horse thief for the captain smiled, nodded and looked very satisfied. At the end of the story he was laughing.

Then it was Hatilshay's turn to speak. He used the Mexican and Chulito gave the words to the captain in his own tongue.

"A friend came to me one day and suggested a raid. A Mexican ranch he said, with many horse . . . ."

"No! Not all of that," Chulito interrupted.

"You are as rude as the Yankee," Hatilshay told him.

"Do not repeat what I have already told him. Yankees will not sit all day to listen. Tell him only how you came into the camp."

From the corner of the tent, the shaman said, "Speak nothing of our having the spirit carving."

Beside him, Turtlehead gave a big sigh. He had limped into the tent with only a little help from the soldier who was not quite a Black Robe. Hatilshay had wondered at his recovery but put it down to Turtlehead's twisted reasoning. He'd probably gotten on his feet to escape the white-eyes so that he could die properly of the stiffness. Or perhaps he did not really wish to die and therefore must return to the shaman for a cure. He was probably telling himself that his strength returned because the spirit carving was removed from white-eye power.

Though his story was now so short that it would insult a gathering of The People, Hatilshay told it. When he reached the place where Poor Lo challenged the white-eye army, even Chulito stared at him in disbelief.

"The old wars were against my people," he said before translating for the captain. "But against the Yankee army it is stupid."

"His way, yes," Hatilshay said.

"Any way."

Hatilshay smiled. "The captain waits. He does not like to sit and listen."

After he'd told of receiving the long eye, Hatilshay added, "I think it must be another of Bobcat Whiskers' jokes."

The Papago nodded. "The paper means the captain must pay for it."

"He must do penance?"

"No, stupid one! He must pay with money. The paper was a requesting slip, or the guards thought it was. It means . . . ."

"It means nothing to me." Interrupting was one white-eye custom Hatilshay found useful, though he would never dare use it among The People.

Chulito grew angry, but not with the interruption. He pointed at the long eye in Hatilshay's hands. "Do you mean to keep it?"

"I gave the paper and received it," Hatilshay told him. "It was a good trade."

"Thief! You are the same as the Yuma!"

There was more before the captain spoke harshly, but Hatilshay scarcely heard. His thoughts were on Chulito's question. Did he mean to keep the long eye? He turned it over, caressing the smooth metal. What a wondrous gift, to see better than others. But would his inner vision then fade? Did it matter? Hatilshay looked to the shaman for help. The old one's eyes held a look Halilshay had never seen. Nor could he read it.

Was the inner vision already gone? Hatilshay suddenly knew its importance. Without it, he could not know what men would do. He'd lost a weapon, perhaps the only real one he'd ever had. He rose quickly and placed the long eye in the captain's hands.

The old one looked pleased and relieved. Then Hatilshay knew what the other look had been. Fear.

He'd failed to recognize it because he'd never thought to see it in the shaman. What had the wise old road-runner to fear? Hatilshay almost laughed aloud. That was the reason. For once the shaman had not known which way Hatilshay would jump. But why should the old one fear a wrong decision? The thought troubled Hatilshay and he pushed it away.

The captain was speaking. When he finished, Chulito grinned and said, "All charges are dropped. My horse is returned to me but the one the Yuma stole remains. The captain says that it is usless to search for the Yuma. He must be far away by this time." He frowned. "Sometimes the captain is too generous."

Turtlehead spoke one of his few Mexican words, "We go?"

"Yes," said Chulito.

Hatilshay went to help the blanket-wearer, but Turtlehead pushed himself awkwardly to his feet, pulled his blanket close and staggered toward the tent flap.

As they stood waiting for the Papago's horse, Hatilshay could not resist murmuring, "There has been a great healing." He wondered if Turtlehead thought the spirit carving already destroyed.

Turtlehead answered eagerly, "The white-eye shaman gave me medicine against the white-eye witch."

The old one's head came up like a dog scenting meat. "A new medicine?"

Turtlehead poured out assurances. "Not a powerful medicine and I am certain it is not long lasting." But he read his uncle wrong. Hatilshay could have told him the shaman wished only knowledge. He grinned as he listened to the old one persuade his nephew to show him this new cure. Before Chulito could say, "Speak the Mexican," Turtlehead was digging in his medicine pouch and thinking it all his own idea. He drew out a square of cloth which he opened to show three round white pellets. The shaman took the cloth, prodded the pellets and smelled them, then passed them to Hatilshay. With only a glance, he handed them to the blanket-wearer.

Chulito leaned close and asked, "Where did you get those?"

Turtlehead snatched the pellets back, folded the cloth and returned them to the pouch.

"Those are the pills the captain makes." Chulito looked from one to the other. "From where did you steal them?"

After Hatilshay explained, there was confusion over who Turtlehead's shaman was. They discovered he meant the holy man Chulito had summoned to help.

Turtlehead said, "When the white-eye shaman came for me, he too was stiff in the legs, so stiff he could hardly walk. Surely it is another of Bobcat Whiskers' spells, but the white-eye shaman has found medicine to take the stiffness away."

"He told you this?" asked Hatilshay.

"He signed, but even that was not necessary. Those under the spell of a witch understand."

Hatilshay turned it all into Mexican for Chulito, who snorted in disgust.

"Spells are a heathen superstition," he said. "The pills remove pain when they are eaten." He pushed close to the blanket-wearer and pointed down his throat. "Eat!"

"Does he think I know nothing?" said Turtlehead. "If I eat the medicine it is gone. This one wishes me to remain as stiff as wood."

He'd spoken in his own tongue but Chulito had not heard. He was greeting his horse like a relative. With a sigh, he waved the blanket-wearer to the saddle. Making a great show of the effort it cost him, Turtlehead mounted.

"The Papago has weakened the medicine," he explained, then glanced at his uncle. "Though it was never strong or long lasting."

As if he hadn't heard, the old one turned to the captain. In the tongue of The People, he said, "Friend." The captain smiled and repeated the word. Chulito took the reins from Turtlehead and led the horse from the camp. Walking beside the shaman, Hatilshay heard the blanket-wearer mutter, "That word was caught by the white-eye's magic drawing. Who knows that it is not touched with their evil?"

His uncle said, "If the white-eye had not known that word, I could not have saved three foolish young men."

His tone warned Turtlehead not to argue, but the blanket-wearer answered, "All the same, words have great power."

Hatilshay could scarcely believe his ears. Turtlehead still thought the same of the white-eyes. Even accepting a white-eye cure had made no difference. He might change his medicine as the spirit carving changed its paint but underneath he remained the same, as stiff and unchanging as the carving itself. To prevent Turtlehead from speaking further, Hatilshay said to the old one, "Tell how you found us."

"When I took the place of the Yuma, someone asked me to chant." The shaman glared at Hatilshay but contined with his story.

The captain had ridden past while the old one chanted. He'd turned back, looked carefully at the shaman and some papers, then called "friend" in the tongue of The People. When the old one answered, the captain dismounted to hunker down and talk. Hatilshay had not given him the words needed so the shaman had drawn a picture of Turtlehead's blanket in the dirt and signed that the wearer was with the soldiers. The captain had spoken to some men, then motioned for the old one to mount one of the pack horses.

"Neither of us knew you and the Papago were also in the camp," he finished.

Hatilshay frowned. "If he came while you chanted, it was but a short time after I left with the Yuma. Why did you not come then?"

"The man the Yuma trades with spoke long with the captain. He was very angry. I think he wanted the soldiers to find the carving. Also, I could not leave until the Yuma returned. I gave my word."

Chulito snorted. "What is the word of the Apache?"

Turtlehead looked down at Hatilshay. "It was as you

said. The Papago sat through the darkness."

"Any time of trouble is a time of darkness." Hatilshay knew the blanket-wearer was deaf to reason but he had to try.

"He sat through the time of darkness," Turtlehead repeated loudly. "I was with him, in the white-eye camp. It was as you said, yet he does not know his friends."

Because he is stiff and unchanging as wood, like you, thought Hatilshay.

"Speak the Mexican!" Chulito softened his voice to add, "It is rude not to. Also, I will think you plot against me."

Hatilshay eyed him suspiciously. A courteous Papago could only be plotting treachery.

They walked in silence to the village. Hatilshay had thought to creep past as close to the river as possible but the shaman led them through a crowd of white-eyes gathered around the store where Poor Lo huddled against the wall. There seemed to be as many white-eyes about as there had been the night Poor Lo led Hatilshay to the village. A man with his face hidden by long black hair kicked Poor Lo and yelled at him.

Though the Yuma must have understood, he answered in his own tongue, then said in the Mexican, "No understand."

After a few more kicks, the white-eye jerked his shoulders and went to stand with a small group of men.

Poor Lo greeted them with sighs and moaning. "Poor trade. All the time, kick Poor Lo, hit Poor Lo. Poor Lo get little food, much hurts."

"Kill that man," Hatilshay advised.

"Maybe. Maybe no." His look of sorrow vanished. "You see steamboat?"

"No." Hatilshay squinted toward the river. "Did it come?"

"Yankees come. Say soldiers say steamboat come. You no see?"

"No, I only said that I saw." Hatilshay explained how he'd tricked the guards into looking away so he could get into the guarded tent.

Poor Lo's sorrow returned. "Yankees much mad. Maybe no food Poor Lo."

The shaman held out his hand. In the palm were silver disks of many sizes.

"Money!" said Chulito. "Where did you steal it?"

The shaman ignored him, speaking to Poor Lo. "When I sat here for you, I chanted."

Hatilshay wondered if he'd ever be pardoned for having made light of the old one's chanting.

"While I chanted," the shaman continued, "many Yankees passed. They dropped these into the basket you had for the mail."

"Truth?" Poor Lo looked as if he'd seen a wondrous vision. "Ha! No more sit, get kicked, little food. Poor Lo chant, get money, much food."

Chulito lifted the money from the shaman's palm. "We need food for the journey home. I will buy it."

Hatilshay was certain the old one had intended the money for Poor Lo, but the shaman glanced at the empty food bags packed behind Turtlehead and said nothing. Chulito gave the reins to Hatilshay and slowly told Turtlehead, "Do not kick my horse. Do not hit my horse. Do not move my horse."

As the Papago disappeared inside the store, Turtlehead said, "He knows his only friend. The horse."

Poor Lo scrambled to his feet and followed Chulito. Before Hatilshay had settled comfortably on his heels, the Yuma was pushed out the door. Poor Lo stumbled, righted himself and came to settle cross-legged beside Hatilshay and the shaman.

"No Indians in store. All the time say Poor Lo steal." He pulled crisp white squares from his rags and crunched on them.

"The Papago is in there!" Hatilshay rose, ready to go to Chulito's aid.

Poor Lo tugged at his shirt. "Yankees say Mexican."

"The Yankees think the Papago is Mexican?" The white-eyes must be very stupid. True, Chulito dressed more like a Mexican or white-eye than did the rest of them but one had only to see him walk to know he was neither Mexican nor white-eye.

"No matter. Yankees hate Mexicans." Poor Lo counted off on his fingers. "There white Yankees, black Yankees, Mexicans and Indians. Yankees hate all the same."

"Even other Yankees?"

"All the same, hate."

Now Hatilshay was certain that white-eyes were many different peoples. But how did one tell the good ones from the bad? He had thought Chulito lied about the numbers of white-eyes in the east but now he was ready to believe at least part. Nor were the white-eyes like any other people. Both Chulito and Poor Lo were right in what they said of white-eyes. Yet both were also wrong. How could one know about white-eyes? Especially the soldiers? It might be of great importance someday. Indeed, it had been of great importance this day.

Hatilshay was explaining some of his thoughts to the shaman when Chulito came from the store to join them. He inspected the horse carefully before taking the reins from Hatilshay, giving him a bulging cloth bag in return.

"Poor Lo go with you," said the Yuma.

"You must wait for the steamboat," Hatilshay reminded him.

"Poor Lo no trade. Poor Lo chant. Get much money, much food." He eyed the bag over Hatilshay's shoulder. "Now Poor Lo go with you."

He followed them out of town, almost treading on Hatilshay's heels. Near the cave they found two of the horses. Chulito whooped, dropped the reins and rushed to greet them. Hatilshay led the horse Turtlehead rode to the cave where he dropped the food bag and helped the blanket-wearer dismount. Poor Lo opened the food bag and stuck his head in. Hatilshay pushed him away.

"Eat now?" asked Poor Lo.

"No." Hatilshay helped Turtlehead to the cave, leaving the food bag in the shaman's care. When he returned for the bag, Hatilshay also brought the leather food bags for repacking. They could be carried behind the saddle easier than the cloth bag. Poor Lo followed, eager to help. Hatilshay gave him a strip of dried beef to keep him away. The repacking was finished before Chulito brought the horses into the cave.

"I could not find one," he said.

"You do not sound unhappy about it," said Hatilshay.

"I had thought to walk home. Still, we are four persons with but three horses."

"I will walk," said Hatilshay. "I feel safer on my feet."

Chulito looked relieved.

The shaman said quietly, "There is still enough daylight to put a safe distance between ourselves and the Yankees if we destroy the carving now."

Poor Lo yelped as if bitten. He pointed to the carving. "You make this nothing?"

"It is the reason we came." Hatilshay tried not to grin. He knew what the Yuma planned. "Shall we burn it?"

Both Turtlehead and Poor Lo shouted protests. Though the carving no longer resembled the blanket-wearer, Turtlehead was not confident enough to risk flames. The old one suggested drowning, which received approval from both Turtlehead, who could swim, and Poor Lo, who must know the river well enough to guess where the carving would come ashore. Hatilshay wondered that Turtlehead did not realize what the Yuma planned, then remembered that the shaman's nephew was blind in many ways. But the shaman must know. And he had suggested the drowning. Hatilshay tried to catch the shaman's eye but the old one avoided his gaze.

As they packed the horses, Poor Lo tried to wheedle more meat. Hatilshay refused him. He knew the Yuma would be trading the carving before sunset. He helped the shaman raise the wooden figure and carry it to the river. Behind them hobbled Turtlehead, leaning heavily on the Yuma. Chulito waited on the trail with the horses.

They placed the carving on its back. As the shaman chanted a medicine song, Hatilshay plastered it with mud. He reasoned that it made the carving appear more dead. Also, it might be harder for the Yuma to find. Adding high wails to the old one's chant, Hatilshay helped him raise the carving. They swung it between them, then let it fly out over the water. They chanted until the current had whirled and bobbed it out of sight. When they turned, the Yuma was gone. Silently, Hatilshay wished him good trading.

Turtlehead rummaged in his pouch, drew out a small brown bottle, drank from it and gagged.

"What is that?" asked the shaman.

"White-eye medicine to take stiffness away. I have saved it, thinking to drink it when the carving was destroyed."

With the shaman's chanting, Hatilshay's mud and the white-eye medicine, the cure should be complete. Hatilshay, walking beside him, sniffed.

"It smells bad."

"Tastes bad. It is medicine of great power." He finished the bottle, tossed it aside and three steps later was vomiting.

Chulito rode toward them, leading the two extra horses. "Now what ails him?"

Hatilshay explained. Chulito dismounted, found the bottle and sniffed at it.

"Stupid one! This is for rubbing on the legs, not for

drinking!" He pushed Turtlehead toward the horses.

"Stupid savage! Do not be sick over my father's horse."

Hatilshay waited for the others to mount. They'd plodded only a few steps when a wailing screech tore the air.

"The steamboat!" said Chulito, fighting his terrified horse.

Two more screeches followed, louder than the first. The horses reared and bolted, proving to Hatilshay that it was better to walk. Turtlehead and Chulito were thrown but the old one held his seat. Even with a horse he knew which way it would jump. But he hadn't known what Hatilshay would do about the long eye.

Hatilshay smiled, remembering. Then he frowned, for again he wondered why the choice had been so important to the old one.

Chulito and Turtlehead were unhurt. The Papago's horse stood nearby but the other had run some distance. Chulito mounted and went to get it.

Turtlehead gazed at Hatilshay almost as he did at his uncle. "You were right. The steamboat came."

Hatilshay did not try to reason with him. It would do no good. What if everyone in the village began searching his words for omens of the future? He would have to be silent forever. Or go among strangers. He turned to the shaman.

"It is my thought that we should know more of the white-eyes. Perhaps I should journey east to their towns, as the Papago did."

He expected the shaman to agree but the old one

argued against it. He even used Hatilshay's own thoughts against him, asking how Hatilshay would know which of the white-eye peoples were good or bad?

"The dangers were the same when you began your journeys, long ago," Hatilshay told him. "But you did not stay by the wickiup."

"I was only a curious young man, wishing to see the other side of the mountain. You are different." He glanced at his nephew and paused as if to choose his words with care. "Not since I was a little boy has there been one who could read the future."

It was true. Many men had a ceremony for curing one illness or finding lost things or game or the enemy. Turtlehead's uncle knew ceremonies and cures for almost all illness, something never before known among The People. Only one who could read the future would be greater. Suddenly Hatilshay understood. The shaman had planned that greatness for his sister's son. He had tried to shape Turtlehead as the white-eye had carved the wood, only the old one had cut too deep. Instead of respect, Turtlehead's constant search for omens brought jokes hinting at a lack of courage. The shaman must have known before anyone else. His inner vision would have seen it.

Then he'd turned to Hatilshay, telling him the old stories, teaching him the Mexican, sharing all he'd learned of other peoples on his journeys as a young man.

"I will go!" Hatilshay was not to be carved by another as Turtlehead had been. He would leave now, before the shaman could mold him into a shaman of great power. But he softened his words out of respect for the old one. "It is in my mind that I should journey among other peoples as you did. Those to the south, the west, perhaps east as far as the white-eye villages."

There was debate, but Hatilshay knew the old one was beginning to think, also, that they should learn more of the white-eyes. Chulito rode up, leading Turtlehead's horse.

"Speak the Mexican," he said wearily.

Hatilshay could not resist telling him, "We speak only of my journey east to the Yankee towns."

"The truth?" Chulito's back straightened and he wheeled his horse. "I will guide you. You will need a guide and someone to speak for you. My father will give us food and horses."

"After we have lost one horse on this journey?" Hatilshay feared such generosity from the Papago.

Chulito grinned. "My father did not expect to see any of them again. It could be that he did not expect to see even me."

Turtlehead mounted. He had folded his medicine blanket and hung it over his shoulder in the way of the Mexicans. Chulito kicked his horse and set a pace he would have complained of bitterly if the shaman had led.

"He is eager to return to the Yankees." Hatilshay trotted beside the shaman's horse. "Do you think I should travel with him?"

"Who am I to council one with the power to see ahead?"

Hatilshay glanced up, expecting to meet the wise

roadrunner look but the shaman stared ahead, his face stiff as if carved from wood. Hatilshay thought of a journey alone with the Papago through strange country.

He asked the shaman, "Will you come?"

"I have made my last journey."

Hatilshay watched Turtlehead lean to inspect the bushes and the ground, searching for omens. What did he know of inner vision, of the reading of men's natures? No wonder that the shaman spoke so little, for who was there to understand? Only Hatilshay.

The horses had slowed to a walk, a pace slower than Hatilshay was accustomed to on the trail. He pretended to be deep in thought until the shaman had dropped a little behind Turtlehead and the Papago.

"A Papago is not the best companion," he told the old one. "I will wait for a time, until I find another."

The shaman said nothing.

"But I will go soon."

Still silence. Was he smiling, thinking Hatilshay was already carved into the form of a wise one?

"I will go," Hatilshay said again, but admitted to himself that he would not leave while the shaman lived. The old one should have a better companion than his nephew.

The blanket-wearer raised his voice. Chulito answered. They screamed blame at each other in four languages. With a sigh, Hatilshay moved to separate them, trying to keep his voice low but firm, like the shaman's.

Afterword

This Much
Is True

In 1858 Jacob Snively discovered gold in Arizona. Twenty-five miles from where the Gila River met the Colorado, Gila City, Arizona's one and only gold town, boomed into existence. In proper gold-town tradition, the best of everything, however gaudy and tasteless, was imported from the East. Unfortunately, the gold quickly dwindled, and in 1862 a flood erased all traces of great and glorious Gila City, metropolis of adobe mansions, tent saloons and stratospheric pretensions. Today the area again produces wealth for Arizonans. Where steamboats floated, ranchers raise lettuce, for the Gila, like the Colorado, has been dammed.

But in this book the river follows its natural course. The country is officially at peace. The Mexican War is over. Its prize, California, is safe in the Union. The New Mexico and Arizona territories, though unwanted, do provide a convenient winter corridor to the Pacific shore. The Butterfield Overland Mail is in full service. A few makeshift army posts give token protection to wagons and immigrants, all headed for California. Few tarry in Arizona.

When the Civil War begins, stagecoaches and soldiers will vanish. At the same time, white-eye stupidity and treachery will decide forever the Apaches' opinion of the Yankee. In the long Apache war, Papagos will scout for the Yankees and help them massacre Apache women and children at Camp Grant. In return, Yankees will dam the rivers, leaving the Papago reservation dry. Underground water will be drained by Yankee ranchers sinking wells just outside the reservation border.

Over sixty years later, the Apaches will build their own dam and be forced to guard it with rifles from "Yankees" in Phoenix.

As for the Yumas, by 1968 less than nine hundred Quechan Indians will remain of over seven thousand Yumans. In that year, the half-starved Quechans will lose their claim to three miles of valuable Colorado River frontage when the government declares it nonirrigable and, therefore, public land. The "nonirrigable" land will immediately be leased to Yuma County for creation of a green and grassy park.

The greatest truths in this book are in the words of Poor Lo.